THE REINVENTION OF THE ROSE

CHRISTINA C JONES

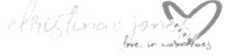

SYNOPSIS

Desperation.

Not a phenomenon Tempest could typically claim, but certainly the catalyst for where she's landed. Not in peril, or pain, but in dire need of the very normalcy she's often emulated, but never been able to obtain.

Now... there's nothing in her way, except all those years of being everything except what she now has to become.

Herself.

As soon as she figures out who that is.

For every one of us who has had to figure out who we are all over again, only to find out she was so much better than expected.

If necessity is the mother of invention, we must consider then,
the impetus of *re*invention.

- CCJ

chapter one

I'D DONE A LOT OF PEOPLE-WATCHING IN MY LIFETIME.

Various reasons came into play with that, most related to the finding of facts, the gathering of information necessary to whatever task was at hand.

Now, when I indulged the urge, it was much less about the utility of it.

It was more to do with the pure curiosity of observing strangers going about their lives.

Without a care.

They were just... living.

Going about their same schedules, their same routines, with zero vigilance.

No real fear of things that went bump in the night.

Or of those things – those *people* - like me, that were stealthy enough not to make a sound.

Not that it mattered anymore.

Not at a time when really, I should envy the overwhelming normalcy of these people – the thing that, for me, had been so damned elusive. Instead of blending in with the crowd, I was relegated to my window, watching.

Well... I guess that implied I *had* to stay there instead of joining in, huh?

In reality, it was more that these people, these days, had exactly no relevance to my life – I didn't fit in, or belong.

A little sad, considering I'd lived in the neighborhood for three months.

Despite the insistence of my mentor, I hadn't been able to bring myself to take advantage of any of the quaint neighborhood's amenities.

Not a single boutique or restaurant.

Not even the coffeehouse across the street.

That was where I saw the most eclectic sampling of the community, streaming in and out of there with hot and cold drinks, pastries in their hands. At night, it turned into a lounge – sometimes with lines reminiscent of a night club, and the throbbing music to match.

I watched.

I listened.

And then one night, finally... I decided I would go.

It took another three weeks to actually go through with it.

Decisiveness had never been a problem of mine – at least not that I could remember. Not until now, when every single one of my own moments was up to me, from the minutiae to the big decisions.

... not that I had many – *any* – of those.

In the immediate, my most significant decision was what to wear to *Urban Grind*, the insanely popular coffeehouse across the street from the abandoned candle shop I'd purchased.

Who the fuck needed an entire storefront for candles?

Certainly not *me*.

What I did need was somewhere that I could fade into the crowd – not so overpopulated that I couldn't be aware of my surroundings, but inhabited enough that I could take advantage of the camouflage that came with living in the "city."

Mahogany Heights was perfect for that.

And so was the apartment above the storefront.

It was studio style, open and airy to make up for the fact that it was tiny, and it was all mine.

There were no wake-up calls, no drills in the middle of the night, no rules – mostly – about what I could and couldn't have.

What colors I could use.

What I could hang on the walls.

What I could have in my closet.

I smirked, very satisfied with myself as I slid the door back on the tiny space, peering in at the hangers that held my curated items. I happened to like the black, white, and gray palette imposed upon us in the *Garden*, so it was repeated here, but still.

I'd handpicked them all, without a single thought to who else might like it.

For tonight's adventure, I chose a simple white top that bared my midriff, comfortable black jeans, and black and white sneakers, and basic silver hoop earrings – I wasn't dressing to impress. I was dressing to look like any other late-twenty-something that might be there, so I could blend into the crowd instead of standing out.

In the mirror, I tugged at the neckline of the top, which I'd never worn before, self-conscious about the tattoo just above my breast, near my armpit.

The only tangible thing linking me to my old life.

It wouldn't do for that to be showing.

Once I was satisfied the shirt did a good enough job keeping my "brand logo" under wraps, I grabbed my keys and wristlet to head out.

This time, I made it all the way to the door that led out to the street before I stopped.

What are you so afraid of?

For the life of me, I couldn't figure it out.

There were very few people in the world who knew who I was, and even fewer cared. Of those who did, maybe some wanted me dead.

Most wouldn't put any money or resources behind it.

My threat level was pretty low.

In fact... I was probably safer *now* than I'd been in a very long time, much more than I'd been when every public outing had a dossier attached, including details of who I was supposed to be at any given time.

I was one girl now.

Just me.

And there was no mission besides living my life however I wanted.

Nobody was coming for me.

And really... maybe *that* was the problem.

I could step, masterfully, into any role I was handed without missing a beat, without detection.

But this wasn't a role.

It was life.

Something I had painfully little experience with.

I pushed the door open and stepped out, refusing to allow myself the comfort of going back upstairs. It was barely ten o'clock, and the spring weather was beautiful, so there were plenty of people out and about.

I ignored them all, locking the door behind me and heading for the crosswalk, keeping my focus narrow.

Across the street.

Through the front doors.

Up to the counter to order a spiked chai with a drizzle of chocolate.

A cozy seat with my drink, close enough to the stage to enjoy the music, but tucked away enough to not be bothered.

You did it.

You're here.

I allowed myself a private smile about this silly ass "accomplishment" before I resumed my usual people-watching, only up close this time. *The Heights* was a majority Black neighborhood, and *Urban Grind* attracted a pretty diverse subsection of that – all ages, interests, economic levels, whatever.

Without even... *trying.*

It was nice.

It was *really* nice, actually.

Especially when I found myself swaying along to the live music, really enjoying it.

This felt good.

The throng of bodies, the loud music, the sweet stench of marijuana faintly mingled with liquor... I couldn't say it was necessarily familiar, but it was comforting. For the first time in a while, actually, there was an unmistakable feeling of ease lightening the usual tension in my shoulders, as I raised my chai to my lips, taking it all in.

Feeling bizarrely guilty about it.

Being comfortable and relaxed, enjoying yourself... those things didn't keep you alive – apprehension and vigilance did.

But... I hadn't been able to exercise even *those* particular muscles as well as I'd have liked over the past year. Though an argument could be made that my persistent caution had kept me safe from the usual harm that came along with my former profession... a somewhat opposite case could be made as well.

A case that I was overthinking this shit.

Because no matter what *could* have happened, if I'd done this thing or that thing differently, the fact was that... there had been no bump in the night.

No one had come for me.

There was no bounty on my head.

No one fucking cared.

For a different woman, that could've been a blow to the ego, but for me, there was a certain freedom in that.

The freedom to sit in a crowded, semi-dark coffee house listening to live neo-soul music that was – despite being embarrassingly cozy – actually... *really* good.

The freedom to just... enjoy myself.

"Pretty bitch like you shouldn't be sitting here alone."

Shit.

Perfection never did last very long, huh?

I kept my face blank as I turned to the man who deemed himself significant enough to interrupt my solitary vibe. Not that it mattered how he looked, what he might have to offer, what-the-fuck-ever.

I wasn't on that right now.

Especially not for a man with *that* haircut.

"No," I said, simply, then tried to give my attention back to my mug.

"Yo, excuse me?" he asked, obviously not getting the picture since he stepped closer.

Rolling my head back in his direction again, I gave him another quick-once over.

In addition to the wack haircut, his clothes were ill-fitting too.

Ugh.

I let out a sigh, resigning myself to the fact that a one-word answer was clearly not enough.

"Stop. Talking. To me."

I let my gaze linger on his, my face pulled into a drab

expression long enough to make sure I'd communicated effectively this time. His brow knit together in a frown as my words connected – *bingo.*

I gave my attention back to the stage, focusing hard on the pretty singer and her pretty boyfriend on the keyboard.

Well... I tried.

Again.

It was hard to keep my focus there when some motherfucker had his hand in a vice grip around my forearm, yanking me up from the bench where I'd been seated and almost making me spill my mug.

It had been so long since I killed a man.

Damn.

I spent a split second erasing my mental *days without incident board*, and then I snatched my arm away from... whoever the hell this dude was, as I struggled to keep myself calm. My mentor would be *really* disappointed in me, if I handled this the way I wanted to.

So I was trying.

"Who the fuck you think you talking to, huh?" His breath was sour with one too many shots as he hissed in my face, obviously emboldened by the darkened room, and the crowd's attention on the stage.

A smile played at my lips as I looked him right in the eyes, deciding right then that I *couldn't* let this ride. "If you don't walk away and leave me alone... a dead man. *That's who.*"

"Ay, what's going on over here?" a deeper, heavier voice broke in, and another man stepped between us, looking in my direction long enough for me to register the *"security"* label printed across the front of his tee shirt. "Are you fucking with her?" he asked the guy, then gave his attention back to me. "Did I see him put his hands on you?"

"Nothing I couldn't have handled on my own," I assured,

looking around him to glare at ol' boy, who was suddenly a lot less bold than he'd been with me.

"I wasn't trying to cause any problems, this bitch just—"

"*Bruh*," Mr. Security interrupted, snatching ol' boy by the collar of his shirt. "You know damn well it don't work like that in here. Let's go," he insisted, practically dragging the guy away.

It only took me a moment to realize that little exchange was garnering unwanted attention, so I wasted no time slipping away before somebody decided to pull out a camera phone.

Something I hadn't even thought about when I was considering killing his ass.

Good thing I didn't have to.

I was waffling on a decision to stay or go when the final notes of music rang out, closing the show. And then the lights were back up, illuminating the room full of strangers and reminding me of where I was.

This had been eventful enough.

It was time to go.

My tea was cold now, but it couldn't hurt to see if I could take one back across the street with me.

"Another spiked chai. To go," I told the barista after I'd patiently waited my turn, then took a seat at the steadily emptying bar until it was ready. Now that the music was done, I assumed they must be closing soon, based on the thinning crowd.

"Sorry about that."

My eyebrow lifted at the sound – and feel – of somebody in my ear, way too deep into my personal space. I turned in my seat, enough to find the security guy standing over me, so close that I could feel the warmth of his body without him actually touching me.

Too close.

"Back up," I said, lifting my hand in a *stop* motion to emphasize my point. The demand made him lift an eyebrow, but he honored it. "What are you apologizing to me for?" I asked, once he did.

"Ol' boy," he answered, with a vague gesture toward the front door. "I saw him approach you... saw you dismiss him. I didn't know he was going to take it where he did."

I shrugged. "So you were watching me, is what I'm hearing."

He smiled, and it was a *very* nice smile.

Full lips, white teeth, the works, especially potent against his rich brown skin.

"What can I say? You're a beautiful woman. So yes, you caught my attention." His eyes were warm, full of interest as he waited for my response – probably expecting me to be flattered by his apparent attraction.

More than anything, I was amused.

"What, exactly, should I do with that?" I asked.

His eyes narrowed, confused. "With what?"

"Your attention. The way you're talking about it, I'm getting the impression it's a high-value item around here, but... I'm not from here. Are you the neighborhood hottie or something?"

He chuckled about that, but... I was serious.

The material was there.

The height, the solid build, the beard, the locs, the full sleeves of ink covering that pretty milk-chocolate skin.

A near-perfect male specimen who wouldn't have been out of place as one of my peers.

"So you think I'm hot, is what I'm hearing," he countered, leaning in even closer.

I smiled at him. "I'm not blind. But I'm also not interested."

"Fair enough," he said, with a respectful nod. "You have a good night."

"You too."

My drink was delivered to me before there was a chance for awkwardness, but before I could pay for it, he stepped in.

"That one's on me, Nik," he told the pretty barista from across the bar, blocking the money I was trying to offer. "Put it on my tab."

"You got it," she answered, smiling, moving on without giving me a chance to protest.

"You didn't have to do that," I said, but he was already backing away.

"I know. Good night," he said again, and then he was gone, leaving me with my gifted drink in hand, feeling... confused.

It wasn't as if it were the first time a man had paid for my drink.

My meals.

My wardrobe.

A foreign property here and there.

That island, out in the Indian Ocean.

I was beautiful, like every other woman who bore the same mark I did, and had been impeccably trained in the art of charming money, information, and any manner of other things out of men.

That was supposed to be behind me though.

And... yeah, this was just a hot tea, but it still felt... weird.

I couldn't dwell on that.

I got my ass back across the street, through the shop, up to my apartment. By the time I got myself back into my comfy lounge clothes, my tea had cooled enough to comfortably sip.

In the window.

While I watched.

Maybe he'd blended in before, but this time, nearly an hour after I'd been home, I spotted him coming through the door. He stood in front of the shop with a group of guys for a while, talking, laughing, just... *being.*

He was beautiful.

I hadn't lied about my lack of interest, but that didn't mean I couldn't look.

I GOT REALLY, REALLY, EXHAUSTED WITH MYSELF SOMETIMES.

It was a state I'd never – to my memory – experienced until this past year or so. Maybe I'd been too mentally occupied before, with analyzing my past performance or planning future excellence, but these days... man.

I was really on my own fucking nerves.

That was the only way, even privately, I could articulate how it felt to be standing in the mirror, the sharpest of my blades in hand, unnecessarily dramatic as I contemplated carving off my rose.

It was ridiculous.

Logically, I knew that, and yet... I didn't feel like I could live with it, a single second longer.

It had been there as long as I could remember, branding me as an asset rather than a fully-realized person. A single red rose, petals beautifully spread and intricately detailed – a loveliness that belied the underlying cruelty it represented.

An exquisite flower, on a dangerous woman I didn't want to be anymore.

Didn't *have* to be anymore.

And yet... I was still marked.

On a deep breath, I lifted the blade to my skin, barely flinching as I pressed it into my flesh. It pricked, yes, but I couldn't bring myself to draw my own blood, even though I'd been trying for the last hour.

Histrionic much?

I tossed the knife onto the dresser, running over the tattoo with my fingers instead. It was flat to the touch, but even with my eyes closed, I couldn't pretend it wasn't there – it was too deeply embedded, in more than my skin.

An ugly stain, in the fabric of who I was.

Yeah.

I can't look at this shit anymore.

I quickly ruled out the knife, knowing damn well I'd never gather the fortitude to flay it off my skin – not under *these* conditions. In some type of high-danger, life or death situation, I'd slice the damn thing off and keep it pushing.

In a reality where I could just as easily walk across the street for a tea and leisurely enjoy it from the comfort of a plush chair in the coffeehouse window without a care in the world?

Not so much.

Full removal required more paperwork and follow-up than I was comfortable engaging quite yet, so it wasn't an option. I knew a few other girls like me, who'd opted for a coverup, and felt at ease with that option.

Now that I'd started making the mental shift from "survive" to "actually have a life" ... maybe that would help me, too.

This wasn't going to be like the pathetic persuading I'd had to go with myself to go to *Urban Grind*.

Nope.

I didn't give myself time to think it over, I threw on some clothes to cover the naked state I'd been in since I exited the shower with slice-and-dicing on my mind.

And then I headed out the door.

DistInk'd was... loud.

Aurally, and visually, both in an aesthetically pleasing way.

The music was loud, the people were loud, the walls plastered in pictures and drawings, several ignored flat screens flashing everything from news to binge-streamed movies and shows. I got a few curious glances as I walked in, but I mostly went ignored except for the girl behind the front counter, sporting at *least* four facial piercings.

She smiled as I approached, putting down her cell phone to give me her attention. "What you need, love?"

"A coverup," I told her, distractedly, as my eyes scanned the wall behind her, taking in what I assumed to be the work of artists on staff. Once my gaze landed on one I liked, I pulled aside the wide strap of my tank top, showing her the rose. "I don't ever want to see this again. And I want to work with whoever did *that*," I said, pointing to a photo of a hyper-realistic koi fish inked across someone's shoulder.

She glanced behind her, her gaze following my directive. "He's gonna be expensive," she warned, once she landed where I was pointing. "Especially for a coverup."

"I don't care," I told her. "Is he here right now? I'll pay extra if I can walk out of here with something new, today."

She raised an eyebrow at me, her gaze falling to where my strap was still pushed aside. "You getting over a bad break-up or something?"

"Yeah. Something like that."

Her pierced lips stretched into a sympathetic smile as she nodded, sliding off the chair to stand. "Aiight. He finished up with somebody else a little while ago. Let me go see if he's up to it."

She disappeared behind a beaded curtain leading into the back of the shop, while I took the opportunity to do a bit more looking around. I had this gran plan to have the rose covered, but no idea what I wanted to be in its' place.

What, exactly would be significant enough to dampen the rose's power?

I wasn't sure.

But what I *was* sure of, was the energetic shift that happened in tandem with the sound of that beaded curtain being pulled back again. I turned around in time to watch the neighborhood hottie make his entrance.

As soon as his attention landed on me, a slick smile spread over his whole face – not just his lips, but the glint in his eyes, the sudden flare in his nostrils.

"This can't be the eager customer, Pri," he said, addressing the girl from the counter as his dark-eyed gaze remained on me. "This woman *isn't interested.*"

My eyebrow went up. "Really?"

"Stop it, Tristan," Pri scolded him as she took her seat back, and picked up her phone. "She had a bad breakup, help her out."

"I didn't actually say that," I corrected, but she was already grinning at her phone, not concerned with either of us anymore. So I repeated it to him, instead, and only got a deepened smirk in return.

"You're not saying it isn't true either," he rightly countered, and I crossed my arms.

"I'm not sure why it matters, at all, anyway. Can you cover my tattoo?"

"I can do anything you can afford."

"I can afford whatever you can do," I responded, already sick of him, from the depth of his eyes to the softness of his beard to the bulk of his biceps, which hadn't been quite so apparent a few nights ago. I pulled my strap aside again, displaying the rose. "Are you fixing this for me, or not?"

His teeth sank into his lip, purposely keeping his gaze locked on mine instead of looking at the tattoo. After a moment, he did, stepping closer to peer at it before he lifted his fingers to my skin, touching me in the same place I'd been sorely tempted to carve off.

I... didn't feel like stabbing him.

In fact, I was drawn to the idea of leaning into his touch, but before that feeling had lingered too long, he'd pulled back.

"It's nice and flat, so that's good. The color is deep and rich – good for a tat in general, but a little more difficult to cover, depending on what you want. You got a picture or something?" he asked, meeting my eyes.

"I don't know what I want."

"Aiight, come back when you do," he said. "We can sketch it out, let you live with that for a few days, then make it permanent."

"No," I said, stepping closer to emphasize how serious I was. "I don't want to come back, I don't want to sketch anything out. I want it tonight. Right now."

"I don't do freehand ink on strangers, sweetheart."

"Name your price."

He scoffed, shaking his head as he took a step back. "It's not about the money. I have a process, and I don't know you like that to be throwing shit off."

"Please?" I asked, disgusted with myself for how desperate my voice sounded but... whatever. "I *need* this," I told him, circling a hand around his wrist as I moved closer, begging with my eyes.

It only took a moment before he blew out a stream of air through his nose, cursing under his breath.

Bingo.

"You don't even know what you want," he accused, in a clear last-ditch effort to get me to leave him alone.

"A storm," I replied, pulling the idea from nothing. "Dark, rolling clouds. Lightning. Sky."

"*Damn*," he frowned. "Not even something simple?"

"Do I seem like a simple girl to you?"

He chuckled, his gaze dropping to where I was still holding on to his wrist. "Nah. You seem difficult as fuck."

"But you're gonna do the tattoo?" I asked, giving him the full-blown puppy-dog eyes I'd never met a man who could resist.

A deep sigh lifted and dropped his broad chest, and he shook his head – not in answer, in resignation.

"Come on back."

"You haven't been drinking, have you?"

I lifted an eyebrow at him as he gestured to the place in his inking room where he wanted me to take a seat.

"No."

"Did you eat before you arrived?"

"Should I have?" I asked, thinking about the big ass honeybun I'd ventured out for to serve as breakfast, and had subsequently served as an all-day meal.

He looked up from a wall of different colored inks he'd been choosing from to tell me, "Yes, probably a good idea. You might be here a while."

Oh.

Good thing I had nowhere else to be.

"How long did the rose take?" he asked, as I shifted my attention to my other surroundings – his private space was much more refined than the general area of the shop. There was the ink wall, a stainless-steel sink and a bunch of storage, a gallery wall of ink I assumed he'd done, and an unfinished mural of a woman's face.

I blinked, realizing I hadn't answered the question. "I can't remember."

Not exactly a lie, but... not quite the whole story, either. I had very specific flashes of that day – the day I "got" my rose, supposedly something to be proud of. None of the details would come through clearly for me though.

"Why no drinking?" I asked, trying to shift the subject.

"Uh... lack of judgment is part of it," he told me, sounding half distracted as he dug through one of the storage drawers. "But mostly, because it thins your blood, makes it harder to get the ink to take, yada-yah."

I watched as he stopped what he was doing to stretch his long, muscled limbs – an act that made me remember what "Pri" said about him before she'd gone to find him for me.

"Am I fucking up your flow or something? You were about to call it a day?"

A grin played on his lips as he kept gathering his tools and supplies in what I assumed to be a sterilized tray. "Nah, sweetheart. Every artist on staff has to put in a certain amount of hours for drop-ins. You got lucky."

"Stop calling me sweetheart."

He glanced up from transferring his supplies to the cart by the table. "What would you prefer?"

"My name."

"Which is...?"

Shit.

I guess people wanted that, huh?

Usually, if I were out amongst the public it was with a firmly planted identity in mind – I wasn't "playing" someone else.

I *was* someone else.

That wasn't an option anymore.

Now, I was just... *me*. Nothing to hide behind, no intrepidly detailed fictional backstory to lean on.

"Tempest," I said, introducing myself by my own name – the only one I'd ever known, at least – for the first time.

He smiled. "Nice. The *"storm clouds"* thing seems much more fitting now. I'm Tristan," he said, offering his hand, which I accepted.

His fingers swallowed mine in a firm grip, and the same *get closer* urge I'd felt earlier returned.

A feeling completely foreign to me.

I didn't let that handshake linger.

If he minded the abrupt way I pulled back, he didn't mention it, dropping onto some strange stool-contraption and wheeling up to where I was seated.

"I'm gonna have you take your arm out of your tank, and your bra strap, if you're wearing one," he said, switching to a very professional, matter-of-fact tone. "I need to shave that area, just in case, and sterilize it, so your clothes might get a little wet. And you might leave here with a bit of ink on them. Is that gonna be a problem?"

I glanced down at my cut-off shorts and the plain tank top I'd tossed on. "No. I can keep my titty covered, right?"

Tristan's eyebrows went up. "Uh... yeah. I mean, unless you want the tat to go down that far."

"No. Just what's needed to cover the rose," I affirmed, then looked up to stare at the black-pained network of pipes that comprised the ceiling.

"You're not gonna run out of here and stiff me, are you?" he asked, in a tone that was only half-joking. "Pri didn't take a deposit, have you sign a waiver or nothing, did she?"

"No. And no. You're not gonna give me a fucked-up tattoo, are you?"

He scoffed. "That ain't even possible, swee—Tempest," he corrected himself.

"Well then... unless you're gonna have me go back out front... I guess we're trusting each other."

I dropped my gaze to meet his, and he nodded.

"Let's get this started."

THE HEAT OF THE NEEDLE AGAINST MY SKIN WAS... BLISSFUL.

With my gaze focused on the gorgeous mural decorating the opposite wall, I forced myself to feel it all – every prick of blazing hot metal, the filling of my pores with ink, the featherlight touch of Tristan's hand as he moved.

As he facilitated step one of my reinvention.

Make no mistake – I was a woman who *required* reinvention. *Intervention.*

There was no real circle of concerned friends or family or coworkers for me, though.

I had to do it myself.

Starting with the obscuring of the red flower that had been part of my identity for much too long.

Burned into my skin, a permanent designation of who I was and why I existed.

A condemnation I'd lived with since... pretty much since I could remember, which wasn't saying much. My very, *very* earliest memories, the ones I could only barely touch, even when I dug for them... they weren't of swings or bike riding or recitals or hanging out with friends at the mall.

They were of the *Garden*.

It wasn't so much that I needed to forget, more that... I needed something else. Different memories, from a different life I had yet to actually *live*.

So, I focused – again, on feeling it all.

Every prick.

I'd gotten much too good at feeling nothing.

Pain was a luxury I'd been mostly stripped of long ago – something to channel into a more beneficial feeling, but never sat with, or explored. Now that I was free to do and think and feel what I wanted... it was mine to reclaim.

As strange as it was.

"Never seen a woman be *this* serene about my needlework," Tristan said from above me. "At least not without a little assistance."

I shifted my gaze from the mural to his face – that *frustratingly good* face.

Dark brown skin, obsidian eyes, that thick, soft-looking beard that would likely feel good against the back of my hand.

Probably even better between my thighs.

"Is that a compliment?" I asked, meeting his gaze. He was looking at me, sure, but also *into* me a little too, in a way that was almost too much.

Almost.

I felt the invasion, but didn't look away.

I waited.

He'd already pulled the tattoo gun away from my skin, but the motor kept buzzing as he stared. "It is."

"Okay. What exactly do you expect me to say?"

"I tend to shy away from those, sweetheart." Without warning, he brought the tattoo machine back to my skin, but I didn't flinch.

Not even because he'd called me *sweetheart* again.

"Away from what?" I asked.

The corners of his mouth lifted in a smirk. "Expectations."

Ha.

He was indulgently tall, sinfully handsome, an immensely talented artist, based on what I'd seen, and in high demand, if I took into account how Pri had been sure to tell me he was expensive.

Of course he shied away from expectations.

"I bet you know a little about that," he said, when I hadn't spoken after a moment. "I get the feeling you defy a few expectations of your own."

"Nobody expects anything of me."

As soon as those words left my lips, I realized how dismal they had to sound. The truth was though, that I wasn't a woman anyone expected anything from, because... I barely existed.

I was here to fix that.

Hopefully.

I closed my eyes, and Tristan took the hint – he didn't ask me shit else, for a while. He focused his attention on my ink – on the intricate detail work involved with turning my rose into a stylized storm, complete with lightning.

The destructive force I was named for.

At least, that was how I always imagined it, since I didn't have a parent or sibling to ask, no box of old letters or archives to pull my history from. For as much as I knew of my own creation, I may as well have been born a fully-formed teenager, with no purpose other than earning and maintaining the rose I was paying some undisclosed sum of money to be delivered from.

Freehand.

I liked the sound of the word – *free*hand. It seemed fitting for the occasion – for the insane amount of gravity it held for me.

"I don't do freehand on strangers," he'd claimed, and yet... here we were.

In a tiny, sterile room, my breast bared down to the darkened fringes of my areola, with some rapper screaming over a beat in the background while I was reborn.

A hundred pricks, and then a wipe away of excess ink, sometimes blood.

Then another.

Then an ink refill, or a color change, and then a hundred more pricks of the needle.

The steadiness, the precision of it all, was soothing.

The sterile gloves covering his hands was a perfect barrier, making it easier to focus on the utility of what was happening, instead of being distracted by his touch.

Though, I'd quickly discovered Tristan was a hard man to completely tune out.

With my eyes still closed, I called his face to mind – I'd already committed it to memory. The wrinkles at the corners of his eyes, the flare of his wide nose, the mid-size gauges in his earlobes, the tiny mole on his top lip – the only slight imperfection to their perfect pink-brown fullness.

And his *arms*.

Full sleeves covered with beautiful ink I hadn't fully examined yet. From my short-term memory, I could pull forth landscapes and flowers, dates and names, faces, military references that made me think that like me, he'd served his country.

I mean… if you wanted to phrase it in such a polite manner.

He wasn't touching me there, but I felt him deep between my legs – *inside* me.

It was… *strange*.

This feeling I'd heard about, been trained to emulate – the kind of profound arousal I'd mimicked but never actually, deeply, *felt*. Not in my time in service to the *Garden,* and not in the time after – the strange, meaningless year without an assignment, without instruction.

Without... purpose.

It was numbing.

Utterly, completely, but with Tristan over me, with his body heat permeating my personal space and the clean, woodsy scent of him filling my nose... I felt something.

Everything.

I opened my eyes, watching his deep level of concentration play across his features as he worked. The pink tip of his tongue jutted from between his lips for a few seconds, and his eyes narrowed, like he'd reached some difficult part. His thick eyebrows knitted together, forcing the wrinkling of his forehead in the middles as he focused.

And then, he caught me staring at him.

Again, he pulled the machine away from my skin as his lips parted, mouth spreading into a wicked sort of smile that had likely wiped away the inhibitions of a long, *long* line of women... maybe right here in this chair.

"What's on your mind?" he asked, studying me as he sat back. This time, he switched the machine off. "You look like you've got something to say."

"Nope. Just observing."

His gaze traveled over me, slow and deliberate.

Heated.

"Seemed like some pretty deep observation."

"Like what you're doing now?" I raised an eyebrow at him.

His perusal of me was far from professional, but I wasn't bothered by that – nor was I surprised. I was well-aware of the effect I had on people – men and women. My looks were a carefully cultivated asset that had served me quite well. A face and body with the ability to straddle the dichotomy between innocently angelic and downright devilish.

And yet, even with this knowledge – this gift, some might call it... I'd never fucked a man simply because I *wanted to*, before.

Maybe I'll start with him.

"What is it that you do?" he asked, finally sitting forward again, ready to work. "Like, for a living. Besides make motherfuckers crash into rocks?"

That made me smile.

He was smart enough to peg me as exactly what I was – a deadly siren, ready to lure men to their deaths – although, of course, he thought it was metaphorical.

"I'm... on sabbatical right now," I told him.

His gaze followed my tongue as I raked it over my lips, one eyebrow hiking as he turned the machine back on. "What does that mean?"

If he didn't have the needle on my skin, I would've shrugged. " that I'm taking a break from it all. To find myself."

"Yeah?" he asked, half distracted by what he was doing. "How is that working out for you?"

"It isn't," would've been the honest answer.

Not even in the slightest.

"I've been adrift, actually," I told him, because he, like everyone else, was a stranger. "No focus."

"I thought the lack of focus was the whole purpose of taking a sabbatical. A... perk."

My gaze drifted up to his again, back to those beautiful dark coffee eyes. "It would seem that way, huh?" I asked, not blinking until he gave his attention back to my skin. We'd been at this for hours, but I refused to look down until it was ready. Until the rose was gone. "I guess... most people would relish the idea of such freedom."

His mouth curved at the corners, white teeth appearing to sink into the soft flesh of his bottom lip, scolding it and suppressing a smile. "You're not most, are you?" he muttered, more to himself than me.

You have no idea.

"What did you do before this?" he asked, reinforcing my feeling that his other question was only barely meant to be spoken aloud. "Before your... *sabbatical*?"

"Followed orders."

He scoffed, chuckling a bit until his eyes drifted back to meet mine, and he realized I wasn't joking. "Really? *You*?"

"Really. Me."

One thick, barely-tamed eyebrow went up. "Wouldn't have thought you were the type."

"What type would you have thought?"

"I told you that already... when I asked about your job before, remember? You were cagey about it then too," he chuckled. "What are you, some kinda secret agent or something? You did pop up in the neighborhood out of nowhere, getting' niggas kicked out of the coffeehouse for coming at you wrong. So really, it checks out."

"Wouldn't I have to kill you, if I told you something like that?" I returned his smile with one of my own, mimicking that lip-bite thing he'd done. "Can you imagine how good I'd look in the outfits?"

"I can," he admitted, after another of those heat-inducing slow perusals. "You still haven't answered my question though."

"I'm retired from my line of work. Prefer to let it stay in the past," I said, in a firm tone that made him nod, and lift his tool again as his smile shifted into a smirk.

"I didn't mean any harm," he told me, after a few moments of silence.

"I didn't interpret any," I countered. "Just... letting you know."

Just... fucking up the vibe, I realized, when he didn't say anything else.

This was the problem, with being in the real world without a yoke.

I wasn't "human" enough, not really, to know how this sort of thing was supposed to go. Not without a dossier with every detail about the man I might need, along with a bunch of shit I didn't *want* to know. Not without a character to portray, or a script to draw from.

There was no guide anymore.

I was just... *me.*

No cues, no applause, no stage direction to let me know if I was hitting my marks.

"Okay... I've gotta go in with some white now, to layer in the details, get a little definition – this is gonna be the worst part, pain wise. I know you're a bad ass and all that, you haven't flinched about the rest of it, but... just a heads up," he said, only giving me a brief glance before his brow furrowed again as he studied his work.

"Thank you," I told him, responding courteously even though I didn't think his little disclaimer was necessary.

It *did* hurt like a bitch.

So much so that I was relieved when it was over, and he sprayed my skin with the bottle from his cart before wiping it one final time, coating it, and then covering with transparent film.

"You ready to take a look?" he asked, already grabbing a hand mirror from his cart, like there wasn't a full-sized one near the door. I opted for the larger one, accepting the hand he offered for assistance from the reclined seat. Carefully, I avoided letting my gaze drift to my fresh ink until I was fully in position, ready to take it all in at once.

"*Holy shit,*" I whispered, once I finally let myself look at it.

The rose was...*gone.*

I stepped even closer to the mirror, as close as I could get without going through the damn wall. You'd think that, having had something on your body for a decade, you'd be able to find it easily, no matter what.

But... no.

Logically, I knew it lay underneath all the fresh ink Tristan had just applied, but from what my eyes were telling me, based on what I could clearly see in the mirror... it wasn't there anymore.

I was as free as the wild fringes of the storm he'd set against the backdrop of a beautifully setting sun – fiery reds and golds breaking through the swirled black and gray accumulations of angry clouds. He'd used negative space, and that painful white ink to create fractured lighting bursts, juxtaposing that destruction against the peace of the sun as it disappeared behind much quieter clouds.

"It's exquisite," I whispered, wanting to touch it, but not daring to disturb it, even though I knew how ridiculous a thought that was.

Just in case, though.

"You're happy with it?" Tristan asked, and I blinked hard, trying to fight back the sudden, unexpected surge of emotion.

I nodded. "Yeah." I cleared my throat, then looked at him in the mirror, not realizing until that moment how close to me he was. "Thank you."

"You're welcome. Ms. *Not Interested*," he teased, breaking the unexpectedly thick tension in the room. "Seriously though... never seen you around here before. You from the city or something?"

"The city?"

"Blackwood," he said, doing that thing again where he

gestured in some nebulous direction like I was supposed to know what that meant.

I did, however, know I wasn't from Blackwood, which was adjacent to the *Heights* – the neighborhood that had been my destination in the first place, by recommendation of my mentor.

"No," I answered, but didn't offer anything else, which made Tristan's smile even broader.

"You're really committed to this *mysterious* shit, huh?"

I returned his grin as I carefully fixed my shirt, taking pains not to disrupt the plastic covering my tattoo. "Yep. How do I settle up my bill? With you, or at the desk?"

"The desk," he answered, tipping his head in that direction. "Pri will get you squared away, and give you a kit with some aftercare information, products, all that."

"Nice. Well... thank you, again, for making the time. And for swooping in the other night, although I could've definitely handle it myself."

He shrugged. "You shouldn't *have* to handle it yourself. Shouldn't have been shit to handle, really, but... such is life, right?" he asked, carefully peeling his gloves off to dispose. "In any case, I was doing my job. On both counts."

"Too many people *don't* do their jobs for that to go unappreciated, so again... thank you."

This time, he nodded. "You're welcome, swee—*Tempest*," he remembered, grinning. "Will you at least tell me if I'll see you around?"

Instead of a direct answer, I hiked my shoulders as I moved toward the open doorframe, knowing now that it was *definitely* time to move on.

"Maybe."

chapter three

RAIN MESSED UP MY PEOPLE WATCHING.

Instead of congregating on the sidewalks and restaurant patios, everybody was driven inside, traveling in cars or under umbrellas, protecting themselves from the late spring downpour.

For three damn days.

Finally, sheer boredom drove me downstairs to the abandoned candle shop I'd been largely ignoring, mostly because it confused me.

What was the point of a whole shop for candles?

It struck me as kinda creepy, honestly.

From the front-facing store portion with all the half empty shelves and dust-covered merchandise wallowing in what seemed to be signature black jars, to the deserted workshop in the back.

There were boxes and boxes of the same jars from the front – empty, of course. Dozens of cartons filled with soy wax that was probably expired, fragrance oils well past the *"use by"* dates printed on the bottoms.

But, even in all its abandoned eeriness... it was kinda intriguing, too.

I opened all the scent oils, breathing them in and almost knocking myself out with the stench of several that had gone putrid. Looked in all the wax cartons, noting how the color of the wax seemed to correlate with expiration dates long passed. I examined the jars of different sizes and shapes, wrestled with spools of candle wick molded together with age. Wondered over what all the different accessories and tools and knick-knacks actually did.

So much shit to make something so simple.

Venturing to the front, I started pulling the cork tops off the already-made candles, curious about the scents chosen for each blend. The labels were all rudimentary, with mostly-faded names that offered no clues about what went in, and without even a proper store name.

Just, *the candle shop.*

"I guess you were really *that bitch* back then," I said aloud... to the store, I guess. And then, "*You are really fucking losing it*," to myself.

Because I was.

I needed to get my ass outta here.

Instead of doing that, I kept opening and smelling candles, until I was satisfied I'd taken in every scent.

There was one that was a clear favorite, and for the briefest of moments I thought about curing my boredom by trying to replicate it.

Then I decided I was probably hungry.

Little by *very* little, I'd been branching more and more into the neighborhood, familiarizing myself with what was available.

There was a *lot.*

Today's interest lied in the restaurant at the fringes of my purview from the window – a spot frequented by locals and visitors alike, who all looked happy and full when they left.

Pot Liquor.

They had food, and I liked food, so... seemed like a match made in heaven.

I went back upstairs for my wristlet and keys, grabbing my umbrella on the way out. It was a wet walk, but in less than ten minutes I was walking through the doors of *Pot Liquor*, having my senses instantly assaulted by... *warmth.*

From all directions.

The rainstorm had brought a distinct chill with it, but the inside of the restaurant was nice and cozy.

And homey.

And bright.

It felt like stepping into a completely different reality from the gloominess outside, and the delicious aromas wafting from the kitchen felt indulgent at this point.

"Hey pretty girl, what can I get for you?" a woman called, from behind the front counter. I stopped my observation of the space to zero in on her – a beautiful woman a few shades lighter than me, with thick short-cropped curls.

More warmth.

"Um... this is my first time here, actually. So I'm not sure," I told her, not fighting the urge to draw closer.

"That's no problem – I've got recommendations, starting with the mac&cheese unless you're lactose intolerant or vegan or something. I made it today, so you picked a good one for your first visit," she told me, lowering her voice for the last part like she was telling me a secret.

Before I could offer any response, a male voice bellowed, "*She lyin'!*" from... somewhere. A moment later, a tall, *fine* ass man came bursting through the swinging doors of the kitchen, scowling at the woman behind the counter. "You think I can't hear you, woman?"

"I think you need to mind your business before you scare off this customer," she countered, the smile in her eyes and on her lips contradicting his glare.

"She ain't scared. You ain't scared, are you?" he asked me, wrapping a big arm around the woman to drag her against his side as she giggled. "Ay, you've gotta come through *tomorrow* if you want the *good* mac&cheese."

"Mixing it up will be your only reminder of a certain sound for a while if you don't *go somewhere*," she said, pinching him, *hard*, under the arm.

"You so *mean*," he yelped, jumping away from her as he rubbed the tender spot. "Hey," he said, addressing me again. "Remember what I told you."

"*Nixon*."

"Okay bye!" he called, disappearing back through the kitchen door as she aimed a swat at him.

"I'm sorry," the woman said, her face flushed with happiness as she turned back to me. "I'm supposed to be recommending a plate for you, not playing around with my foolish husband."

I shook my head, returning her smile. "No, it's fine. Y'all are sweet," I assured her, not bothered in the least by their display. If anything, it was a bright spot in this gloomy ass day, seeing their natural chemistry.

The kind of love I'd feigned for the purposes of a mission, but never *actually* experienced before.

That whole interaction could've been pulled right from a training video.

"Did you want to try the mac?" she asked, taking us back to the matter at hand. "If you eat meat, we can put some fried chicken with it, some greens, some yams..."

"Yeah that sounds amazing, sign me up."

She grinned. "I gotcha sis."

I paid for my meal and then ventured to the open dining area to take a seat. It wasn't prime lunch time, so it was semi-empty enough for me to relax and let my mind drift.

Back to the candle shop.

Damn that space for being so intriguing, cause now I was wondering about it. Well… daydreaming, really.

I didn't need money, thankfully, so I didn't have to give a job much consideration. The work force was *not* ready for me, nor was I ready for it.

I had some acclimating to do first.

What I *could* use, was a hobby – one I could safely engage from the privacy of my own space, without anybody getting into my damn business. Honestly… I was getting a little excited about the thought of figuring out the whole process without much instruction, blending and formulating my own scents.

I did good with something to focus on.

Unfortunately, the bell over the front door drew my attention, breaking me away from my thoughts. My eyes instinctively went to the new arrival, going wide for a moment at the familiar sight of locs, a beard, and dark bronzed skin.

Tristan.

I watched, enthralled, as he interacted with the woman behind the counter – *Charlie*, according to him. They talked and laughed while he ordered his food, their conversation drawing Nixon back out to the front to join the fun for a few moments before Tristan moved on, to take a seat and wait for his meal.

I'd already looked away, pretending to bury my attention in my phone, but of course he spotted me.

"*Ms. Not Interested,*" he said, and I looked up in time to see him taking it upon himself to slip into the seat across from me in the booth I'd claimed. "So I *did* end up seeing you around."

I shrugged. "That's not really a great feat, since I *do* live in the neighborhood. Also, you know my actual name, so..."

"I do," he conceded, his lips spreading into a grin that brought inappropriate things to mind. "But I *so* enjoy reminding you of that, since you did, indeed, end up quite interested."

"In your talent as an artist. Not your dick," I said bluntly, even though I was, actually, very much interested in that.

"Fair enough. Although..." he glanced around, then leaned across the table a bit. "You should know... I'm about forty percent sure you're actually trying to convince yourself of that."

I smirked. "Forty? That's pretty damn confident."

"I think it's pretty solid too. Am I right?"

"This wouldn't be much fun if I just *told you,* now would it?" I asked, lacing my fingers together and propping my elbows on the table as I leaned in a bit myself. "You'll have to figure it out. And risk me stabbing you in the process, if you're wrong."

One eyebrow shot up. "Stabbing? Damn. I know you're mysterious and all, but..."

"You're the one who sat down to flirt with a stranger," I reminded him, glancing up as a staff member brought out my food, which I'd luckily ordered *to go.* "Don't act scandalized now."

He chuckled. "Nah, that's not it. I'm just not sure what it says about me that the threat of being stabbed has me even *more* interested in your lack of interest."

"You should examine that," I said, rising with my food tucked in one arm, umbrella tucked in the other. "By yourself."

I left him sitting there laughing, knowing he couldn't follow me without leaving his own food behind – and as good as this place smelled, he wasn't doing that.

The endless storm had picked up, so I spent a few moments underneath the awning outside the restaurant getting myself situated – wristlet and food secured, umbrella held high to protect from the elements.

That didn't last long.

I'd barely made it half a block when a sudden, heavy gust flipped my umbrella inside-out, making a complete mockery of the "heavy duty" claim that had been all over the packaging. Foolishly, I struggled with it for a few moments, working to get it flipped back into the right position while huge drops of rain pelted me from what seemed like all sides.

Finally, after a couple of tries, I managed to flip it back the way it was meant to be.

Only for it to happen again a few steps later.

"*Goddamn it!*" I yelled... at the weather, I guess, only to hear a rumble of laughter start up from behind me. When I turned around, Tristan was sauntering in my direction, food in hand, holding an umbrella that looked a helluva lot more *heavy duty* than mine.

"You look like you could use somebody to come to your rescue," he teased, holding his big ass, tough ass umbrella over both of us. "You're lucky the hail already passed."

I blew out a sigh, dumping the useless combination of metal and cutesy fabric in a nearby trashcan before wiping my face dry with the sleeve of my hoodie. "Thank you," I told him, peering at my bag to make sure my food was still safely secured in the recyclable containers it all came in. "I've never had that happen to me before."

"I could tell," he chuckled. "I've got you from here."

Immediately, I shook my head. "You don't have to do that," I said. "Going out of your way."

He shrugged. "You passing UG?"

"The coffeehouse? Uh... yeah."

"That's not out of my way at all then. Let me at least get you there."

He didn't wait for an answer.

He switched the umbrella to the same side where his food was looped over his arm and put a hand at the small of my back, easily steering me like we knew each other.

Entirely too familiar.

I wanted to mind it, a lot.

The fact that I didn't made me temper my reaction, simply moving away from his touch without mentioning it. I really didn't want him walking me "home" either, but if he was already going that way I wasn't about to get soaked for the fun of it.

I also wasn't about to argue while my food got cold.

"How is the tat?" he asked, breaking the silence between us. "You still happy with it? Feeling good about it?"

I haven't wanted to carve off a chunk of my skin even once since I got it was the real answer, but since I didn't think that would go over well, I nodded.

"I'm happy. Thank you again."

"You ain't gotta thank me, sweetheart. It was a nice challenge," he explained, stopping to wait for the crosswalk signal before we crossed the next street. "Felt a little bad covering up your other work. Must've been an ugly breakup."

"Very." As soon as the *walk* signal popped up, I moved, with Tristan falling into step right beside me. "Nightmare inducing."

"Damn. Was there like... abuse or something?"

"You're nosy," I said, stopping in my tracks to face him directly.

"My bad. I prefer to think of it as simple curiosity. Power of deduction."

"What does that even mean?"

"It means... shit, if I'd left an abusive relationship I'd be getting new tats and being a mystery person too," he shrugged.

I met his gaze, considering his words – the accuracy in his framing of a past he knew nothing about. "Yeah. It's cool."

"It is?"

"It is," I nodded, turning to start walking again. "Because I will never, *ever* be controlled again. By anybody. So I'm good."

I had a hard time meeting his gaze after that, knowing he was probably wondering what the hell was wrong with me, and what was happening in my head. So I didn't even try, opting instead to focus on getting back to the candle shop.

A mistake I didn't realize until I was standing in front of it, with my keys out.

A mistake I *never* would have made before my abrupt departure from service to the *Garden*.

"This is your spot?" Tristan asked, incredulous, as he peered through the dust-coated glass, trying to get a peek inside. The awnings were cared for by the neighborhood as a whole, so they were still intact, giving us the protection needed for him to let down the umbrella.

I had my keys out like a dummy, so there was no point in lying.

"Yeah," I told him. "That some kinda problem?"

He shook his head. "Nah, not at all. Just... unexpected. Which I... should've expected, honestly," he chuckled. "You gonna revamp it or something? You really like candles?"

"I don't give a shit about candles," I blurted. "But... yeah. I might revamp it."

"Why spend the time on something you don't give a shit about?"

I shrugged. "Why not?"

"Because you could spend it on something you *do* give a shit about it."

"But I don't have anything I give a shit about," I argued, immediately regretting my candor when I saw the way his expression changed. "I mean... I don't *know* what I give a shit about," I corrected. "I didn't... I didn't have a lot of leisure time, before I left my job."

"*Ohhh*." His face relaxed, and he nodded. "That's right, you did say you were on sabbatical. That's a lot of change at once," he added. "Breakup, leaving your job, starting a new thing, getting tattoos, threatening to stab niggas... I'm no expert, but it seems like you're beasting this whole *woman of mystery* thing."

I laughed, shaking my head at his assessment of it all. Of course I couldn't correct him about the breakup and the job being related to the same thing, but I couldn't front... it felt good to have someone thinking I was getting something right.

Especially since it didn't feel that way to me.

"I'm glad you think so," I told him. "But... I think our food is getting cold."

"It reheats fine," he countered with a grin, then bit his lip. "But I'll let you get to it. *Ms. Glad You Think So.*"

"Oh, so I'm not *Ms. Not Interested* anymore?"

"Nah, you're way too interested for that."

My eyebrows shot up. "Oh, you think so?"

"Nah, I *know* so," he said, letting his umbrella out again as he backed away. "I'll see you around." He stepped from underneath the awning, still looking at me, but then shifting back to the store window. "*Candle shop*," he muttered, like he could barely believe it. "What are you gonna call it?"

I looked at the window, considering the question for a moment before I shrugged.

"I'll be sure to let you know, when I know the answer to that."

chapter four

D𝚘 you really think you'll ever be more than an asset?

A puppet?

You can't possibly believe you'll ever be able to function without someone else pulling your strings.

Stupid girl.

Those were the thoughts that woke me from my sleep in the wee hours of the morning, driving me from the warm comfort of my bed. It was frustrating, really, because sleep was already a scarce resource for me – one I refused to augment with artificial means.

Even if it meant I'd be dragging ass for the rest of the day.

It wasn't as if I had any place to be anyway.

Phone in hand, I went downstairs, to the workroom that was now pretty empty. After a deep dive of research – the one plus side of my insomnia – I'd gotten rid of all the old expired wax, fragrance oils, old candles and everything else that was no longer usable.

And ordered all new things.

Fresh soy wax flakes and wood wicks that would crackle like

a fireplace when burned. Essential fragrance oils, and thermometers and all kinds of other shit.

I kinda needed an obsession – somewhere to focus my energy and attention that was... *healthy.* And I'd found one.

None of the new things had arrived yet, though.

So, I sat down in the middle of the empty workroom, imagining what it could be, and marveling at the fact that I.... was really about to make fucking candles, of all things.

Chuckling to myself, I picked up the phone and unlocked the screen, dialing my mentor's number. It was early – or late, depending on how you looked at it – but before she'd sent me here, she'd insisted on something.

If you need me... call me.

So I did.

"Are you okay? Did something happen?" she asked, picking up after the second ring. She sounded breathless, but not in *ran to the phone* kinda way – a suspicion furthered by a male voice mumbling in the background, far too close for him to *not* be intimately near.

"No. Not really. I'm fine," I quickly shot off. "Is this a bad time? Because—"

"No," she insisted. "Will you get off me?" she hissed, half-annoyed, half-giggling, in a damn-near identical tone to what Charlie had been using with her husband in *Pot Liquor* last week.

That *in love* sound that grated at me.

"Are you sure?" I asked, not wanting to interrupt, and also not wanting to hear her go back and forth with her lover about whether or not he was going to give her any peace.

"Yes," she answered, clearing her throat. "Cree is going to behave himself—"

"Hey Tempest!" he called in the background, and despite myself, I smiled.

He was cool.

And *fine*.

"Tell him I said hello," I told Alicia, and she delivered the message before demanding that he *really did* leave her alone, this time.

He promised.

And then he made her giggle again.

Giggle.

As if she wasn't one of the deadliest *Roses* the *Garden* had ever seen, damn near a legend before she left to re-integrate into "normal" society. We were only *Roses* at the same time for the briefest of periods, but I, like the other girls, idolized her.

Romanticized her story.

The truth was ugly though.

I only *barely* blamed her for upending my entire life by bringing the *Garden* down.

"Assuming you're still in *Blackwood*, you're what, three hours ahead of me? So you should be good and sleep right now, but you claim there's nothing wrong?"

Her mention of the time difference made me not feel as bad about calling at this time – it wasn't as odd of an hour for her as it was for me.

"There's *not* anything wrong," I insisted. "I can't sleep."

"You called because you can't sleep?"

"I called because I'm going to make candles."

There was silence on the other end of the line for a moment, and then a quiet, happy chuckle. "You found your hobby."

"I did."

"Good. *Good*," she repeated. "Does that mean you're getting settled in pretty well?"

I shrugged, as if she could see me. "It's fine. I guess. I got my tattoo covered."

"Really?"

There was a hint of surprise in her voice, but no judgment. We'd talked, at length, about the mental block she'd had for so long about having hers covered or removed – a decision she'd come to realize was for the best.

And... maybe it was.

If she hadn't been able to show it to me when she requested to meet with me, to help *me* transition as successfully as she had... I wasn't sure I would have trusted her.

Hell, I wasn't sure *now* that I trusted her.

But that rose made her the closest thing I had to family.

"Yeah," I answered, after a deep sigh. "It was either that, or I was going to end up carving it off."

"I'm glad you went with a healthier option. What did you get it covered with? Does it look good?"

"It looks great," I admitted. "It's beautiful. The artist who did it, he... he did a wonderful job."

"Hold up – what was *that*?"

My eyebrows shot up. "What was what?"

"Your whole entire tone changed when you mentioned the artist."

"Did it?!"

It was an earnest question.

Tristan and his beautifully inked biceps *had* flashed in my mind, but I didn't think—

"Yes, it absolutely did," she laughed. "So... spill the beans. You met somebody?"

"I've met a lot of people," I lied, and she knew it, because the next thing out of her mouth was a scolding. "*Fine*," I admitted. "The guy who did the tat for me... he's been... not horrible to run into."

So *not horrible to run into* that I'd actively avoided it since the day he and his umbrella had rescued me from the rain.

"Is it serious?"

"There's no *it* for *it* to be serious," I told her. "I'm not... I'm not ready for anything like that. I'm not ready for anything at all."

"Are we *ever*?" Alicia asked. "I mean... listen, I'm no expert, at all, right? But I do know that this – you figuring out how to live your life for yourself – is not a mission. There are no briefings, no run-throughs, no drills, no... instructions. You'll never be *ready*. You're going to have to dive in and make some mistakes."

"Mistakes get you killed."

"Not so much anymore. That's *Garden* mentality seeping through," Alicia warned. "Obviously, I get it – I mean, I have a whole security firm, so it's not like I don't understand the presence of danger, but... again, this isn't a mission. Your neighbors aren't enemy combatants. You don't have any targets except... living a good life."

"That shit is *so* easy to say," I groaned.

"You think I don't know that?" she countered. "Have you forgotten that I was in your exact same shoes?"

No.

I hadn't.

It also hadn't escaped my notice that she was being *very* generous with the "exact same shoes" thing. The truth was that she'd had it harder, having to assimilate into a whole new role without at *least* the benefit of knowing she wasn't alone in her... confusion.

There were women – and men – in the same predicament as me, all over the world right now.

Without the benefit of a mentor who actually "got" it.

"You know... maybe we're going about this the wrong way," she continued, when I hadn't answered. "When I first left the *Garden*, the Whitfields sent me to therapy, which was a double-edged sword. It helped me be able to cope, but... I still had to pretend to be something I wasn't. I couldn't open up to anyone, even my therapist, about the things I'd done. I had to fake it."

"What are you saying?"

"I'm saying... maybe it would be more productive for you to step into a role. The role of who you *want* to be. Deep cover."

"I don't want to live a lie."

"I know," Alicia agreed. "And I don't want you to either – I want you to *live*. But to get there... you might have to fake it until you make it. What you *want* is to be a normal young woman, who makes candles and has a crush on a guy. And makes friends, and maybe forms a romantic relationship, and starts a business, and... doesn't have the urge to kill people. Doesn't have nightmares about it. Right?"

I blew out a little sigh, then nodded. "Right. I guess all that would be fine."

"Okay, so... you've gotta move on that. You've gotta step into the role of a woman who *does* those things, not one who watches others make them happen. Don't think about – *do it*. Be that girl until you *are* that girl."

"That feels like cheating."

"Who gives a fuck?" Alicia scoffed. "Obviously, you're going to do whatever you want – I'm just offering my advice. I'm not your handler, Tempest – I'm your friend. It's been over a year, and yes, you've made some strides – I don't wanna discount that. But if you're telling me that's not enough for you, that you want more, that you're tired of just... existing? You're going to have to change something."

"*How*?" I asked, shaking my head. "I hear what you're saying, but... *how*? Every conversation is so awkward, and stunted, and I know the people around here think I'm some weirdo."

"I doubt it," Alicia laughed. "I'm sure it feels exaggerated to you, but... you were a *Rose*. Does that have to define you? No, of course not. But you don't have to act like your past didn't leave you with a certain skillset – one of them being the ability to improvise, and talk your way through a situation. You can walk into any room and adapt. You can have a conversation with *anyone*. Don't be so consumed with becoming someone new that you feel like you have to suppress even the good parts of who you already were."

"Okay mom."

Again, she laughed, not bothered by my dry tone because she knew – like I did – that she was probably right.

I'd spent the better part of a year drifting until, through mutual contacts, I heard that Alicia was looking to connect with any "stray" *Roses* who needed a place to land. And even after that, I hesitated to reach out, unsure if I could trust her, or anyone.

It took a while for me to come to the realization that... I kinda had nothing to lose.

I didn't lose though.

Even with all the uncertainty, it felt, to some degree, like I'd won.

I was free, mostly, to do what I wanted.

It was a point now of really figuring out what that was.

And... doing it.

"Dacia and Pen will be happy to know you called. They've been asking every other day. You do have their numbers, right?"

I sighed. "Yeah. I do."

"Just making sure. Since I asked them both to give you space to make first contact, and... I dunno, talk? Be friends?"

I let out another sigh. "Yeah. Maybe."

Maybe if they didn't remind me so much of what I'm trying to get away from...

"Don't let me pressure you," Alicia insisted. "Just... remember that you're not as alone as you might feel. Or rather... you don't have to be."

"I hear you."

"That's all I ask."

We said our goodbyes from there, and I got off the phone... feeling good that I'd called. Was I going to call or text Penelope or Dacia, both of whom I'd been at the *Garden* with?

No.

At least, not today.

But it *was* comforting to be reminded that I had the option.

I spent some time cleaning, and researching more about this whole candle thing, and obsessively tracking my supply orders. Finally, once an acceptable hour for it had been reached, I donned some *actual* clothes and made my way across the street to the coffee house for the tea I'd taken to getting every morning.

Even though I should probably know better than to form a routine.

My lack of sleep had caught up with me, and I needed a remedy for that.

The weather was much improved over what it had been for the last week or so. The rain had finally broken, giving way to beautiful sunny weather that had people out breathing it all in – including, apparently, my neighbors.

"You must be the lil' cute weirdo Keem was telling me about," I heard shouted at me, as soon as I stepped from underneath the awning.

Shielding my eyes from the sun with my hand, I peered around until a raucous chuckle drew my attention upward, to the balcony above the store front next to mine, where a fair-skinned man was sitting, shirtless, cocktail in hand.

It's not even seven in the morning yet.

"Um... I guess so?" I answered, making a snap decision to actually follow Alicia's advice and try to engage people more.

And since I did know who "*Keem*" was.

I'd met him pretty shortly after moving in – inevitable, since he owned the storefront directly next to me – an atelier and styling service. I knew from personal experience that could go one of only two ways – men who cared about clothes were either insufferable or *great*, no in-between.

Luckily, Keem seemed great.

I could only guess that the shirtless, light-skinned man of obvious leisure on the balcony was the husband he'd mentioned when he introduced himself.

Carlos.

"Nothing wrong with being weird – these regular motherfuckers are boring," he called down to me, then took another sip of his drink. While I watched, he sat forward, lowering his shades to peer at me. "He was right. You're gorgeous. You're not wasting that face and body *not* being somebody's sugar baby, are you?"

I laughed, shaking my head. "As a matter of fact, I *am* wasting this face and body on exactly that."

"Mmm," he exclaimed, shaking his head. "Damn shame. If I looked like you, I wouldn't pay for shiiiiit."

My eyebrows went up. "You're definitely prettier than me."

He snatched his shades off to grin down at me. "I like you bitch."

"Thank you, I think."

He tossed me a wave, and then went back to… tanning, I guess. Whatever he was doing, I was clearly dismissed, so I returned to my business of getting across the street, and into Urban Grind, which was already packed.

Prime people watching material.

I made a quick decision that instead of leaving with my drink, I would actually stick around, finding myself a quiet corner. Halfway through the line, I heard my name called, bringing an instant frown to my face as I peered up to the counter, where the woman I'd identified as a manager was holding up a cup, and looking straight at me.

"Tempest – I've got your Mocha-Matcha Melee ready."

Confused, I stepped out of line to approach Anika – that was her name, according to the badge pinned to her chest. "Um... I haven't even ordered yet..."

"Yeah, but you get this every day... unless you were switching it up?"

"No," I admitted. "I guess it didn't occur to me that anybody was paying that much attention to me."

I definitely should've.

"We make it a point to identify our regulars," she grinned, handing me the cup. "No creepiness intended."

I shook my head. "It's fine, really. At least I don't have to wait in line. It's three-eighty-two, right?"

Her grin stretched wider. "You're already taken care of, actually. Tristan had me put you on his tab."

Really?

Unbidden, a smile came to my face before I mentally smacked it back down, realizing that shit like this was... exactly what I didn't need.

Probably.

"*Motherfucker*," I grunted, and Anika's eyes got big, the grin dropping from her face.

"Ah, hell – I thought it was a cute thing since he obviously likes you, but I'm not accidentally helping that nigga with any stalker shit, am I? Cause I can have his ass kicked for you. It might take a few people," she murmured, frowning as she really considered it.

"No, nothing like that," I quickly cleared up, before she took those thoughts too far. "It's not really a problem. I ... I'm... *shit*."

"Not sure about him?" she asked, leaning over the counter so she could lower her voice. "If it helps, I've not heard anything *bad* about him. He's only lived here a few years – *Blackwood* transplant. He does security for us a couple nights a week. Cute. Funny. Never seen him on any disrespectful or inappropriate energy, all that. He's cool."

"Yeah… I don't know. He's a little *too* fine. Too smooth."

Anika nodded, laughing as she straightened up. "I will not front like I don't understand *that*. I spent as long as I could dodging it, personally, so… I get it. But… you paying for your own drinks, or running *his* pockets?"

"He got it," I answered, joining her in a laugh before I moved on so she could get back to her job.

Just like I'd planned, I found myself some solitude in a cozy corner and planted myself there.

To watch.

For so long that I got desensitized to the bell over the door, because there was so much more to look at.

Well.

Until *he* came through the door.

With his arm wrapped over the shoulder of a much younger woman.

Actually… not a woman at all, even though she was tall.

A fucking *teenager.*

The youth in her face told the real story as Tristan leaned down to speak into her ear, saying something that made her burst into laughter, showcasing hot pink rubber bands on her braces. I was already out of my seat, my face hot with rage as I gripped my empty mug, thinking about how much force I'd have to use to put it through his temple.

She couldn't be older than *maybe* fourteen.

Maybe.

But then Tristan looked up.

Noticed me.

Smiled.

Said something to the girl who was way too young to be with him, causing her to look up too – she, as opposed to him, shrank away.

"Daddy, she looks like an assassin."

Tristan scoffed. "See? I told your mama you watch way too much damn Netflix. An assassin, really?"

"*Look at her face.*"

I could hear their conversation, of course, but my mind was still stuck way back on one word.

Daddy?

"You have a kid?" I finally said out loud, some of the tension leaving my shoulders.

His eyebrows went up. "Yeah. Temp, this is Kiara. Kiara, this is Tempest. I told her about your storm tattoo," he explained.

"*The assassin tattoo,*" she muttered, and he nudged her in her side, hissing *stop* at her.

"Why are you calling me *Temp*?" I asked.

"You don't like it?" his forehead wrinkled in... *adorable* confusion. "I thought it was cute."

"It *is* cute," I agreed. "Do I look like a *cute* nickname kinda person?"

A smirk spread over his lips. "Actually, you--"

"Don't fucking say it!" I hissed, then immediately pressed my lips together, embarrassed, for cursing in front of his kid. I glanced at her, then back at him. "Sorry."

"She's not sorry, Daddy. She's definitely gonna kill you," Kiara murmured, shaking her head.

"I'm not gonna kill anybody," I defended, only *half* remembering this kid didn't actually know what I was.

What I *used* to be.

I didn't *think* I was gonna kill anybody...

"Don't pay her any mind," Tristan said. "It's the tween imagination – overactive and getting the best of her."

Kiara crossed her arms, lips pursed. "If you're not an assassin, why are you dressed like one? It's *spring*."

My gaze dropped to my clothes, and I *almost* smiled, but I held it back before I looked up again, meeting her eyes. "Fair point," I admitted, since my black crop top, black leggings, heavy black boots and ponytail were pretty much a television super-spy uniform. "I like black. I'm not an assassin. Would an assassin drink out of this cutesy mug?"

"Yes," she nodded, looking *just* like a pretty version of her father.

So much so that it was embarrassing I'd thought it was anything else at first.

Perils of being exposed to a constant parade of the absolutely worst in humanity, for so long.

"How can I prove myself?" I asked her, not even knowing why it mattered, but... it did, kinda.

"You can't. The more you prove you aren't, the better your cover must be," she shrugged, then looked to her father. "Can I get back in line for my lemonade?"

"Yes," Tristan sighed, shaking his head. "But hurry up, so we can get you to school."

She opened her mouth to say something else, but Tristan gave her a look of censure I never would've known he was even capable of if I hadn't seen it for myself. Kiara trudged past us, muttering more about *assassins making her late* – an insistence that might've concerned me a little if Tristan didn't say...

"Please don't mind her – she's been watching some spy shit she's *really* not old enough to be watching, and she's obsessed," he explained, shaking his head. "Her and her mom."

"How old is she?" I asked.

"Thirteen. Going on goddamn twenty."

I met his gaze. "And how old are *you*?"

He blinked, the briefest flash of shame crossing his face

before he answered the question. "Thirty. Yes, I had a kid young, but we're doing right by her, which not everybody can say."

"Are... you really used to being judged about that or something?" I asked. "Cause... you don't have to be defensive about it. I was just asking, because I didn't know. You *don't* seem old enough to have a teenaged kid, but I don't mean that in a bad way. And I didn't mean any harm."

Running his tongue over his teeth, he nodded. "Yeah... my bad. I *am* used to people getting weird about it, so... yeah."

"You good?"

He smirked. "I'm good. *You* good?"

"I'm great," I answered. "Thanks for the drink," I said, holding up the mug he'd come close to having put through his head. "I *really* don't need that, though."

"Not about what you need. Did it make you smile?"

Instead of answering, I dropped my gaze, which only made him chuckle.

"See... you can't even help yourself," he teased. "What are you doing tonight?"

My eyes shot up. "What?"

"What are you doing tonight? As in, with your free time, after eight o'clock? It's open mic. You should slide through."

I frowned. "I don't... *hm*."

I had to stop short of saying I didn't think I would be into it, because... I kinda didn't know what *I* was into. I had to experience it, to figure that out.

"I'll think about it," I told him, earning myself a grin and a parting wave before he moved on to join his daughter.

And then I moved on, back across the street, back to the sweet solitude of my apartment above the shop.

I had no problem finding sleep this time, even with the caffeine in my system.

It had been an eventful morning for me.

chapter five

I should've asked if this was like… a date.

It couldn't be, right?

I'd told Tristan I would *think about it*, and he'd been fine with that answer, because he would be at Urban Grind tonight either way.

My presence – or absence – wouldn't have any real effect on his night.

So… definitely *not* a date.

Establishing that in my mind was of zero consequence, I realized, as soon as I eliminated the possibility as an excuse. *Still,* even knowing this was something casual…

I had no idea what to wear.

What would Dacia do?

I blinked as those words flashed in my mind – a common refrain she'd insisted upon back in the *Garden*. Often, she would curate the wardrobes the *Roses* under her tutelage traveled with, or whatever items were in our cover identity's closet. When we went out into the world, without the luxury of having her over her shoulder, we had a very specific guiding light – *What would Dacia do?*

Hm.

She... would dress like it was a date anyway.

So that's what I did.

Skinny jeans and heels, and a top that hung off one shoulder – showing off my tat, and freshly washed and blown out hair. Red lips, lots of mascara, big silver hoops.

Dacia would be proud.

Open mic started at eight, Tristan had said, so I waited until precisely eight-twenty-eight to step out of my door. Like earlier, the weather was pleasant and warm, punctuated with enough of a crisp breeze to make it – to me – perfect.

Already, this was going well.

Across the street, I slipped into the crowded coffeehouse, knowing my chances now of getting a quiet spot to myself were slim to none. It struck me, quickly, in this room full of strangers how massively alone I was.

And how vulnerable.

"Hey, you made it!"

I barely had time to register his voice before Tristan's hand was at the small of my back, serving as the early warning that he was approaching me from behind. His arms wrapped around me in a hug, pulling me into the warmth of his body, surrounding me in the clean smoky-sweetness of his cologne and... something else.

I couldn't focus too much on it at the moment, not with his fingers laced through mine, tugging me to *"Come on, we've got a table."*

I didn't know who *we* was, but I went along with it, still dazed by both the familiarity of the way he'd greeted me and the fact that I'd kinda enjoyed it.

More than *kinda*.

We, apparently, was a small collection of people Tristan

knew, some of whom I'd seen in different places across the neighborhood as I forced myself to venture out more and more. He introduced me to them in a blur of names and faces I was too staggered to retain, then pulled me into seat beside him in the booth.

Like it was some kinda norm.

"You look good as *fuck*," he said, his eyes noticeably low as he pulled back to stare. "I see you've got my ink on display."

"I do," I told him, my own eyes narrowed as I tried to figure out what was different about him, because there was *definitely* something. I leaned in, taking a deep inhale, and just like that, I figured it out, meeting his gaze with a smirk. "You've been smoking, haven't you?"

His face cracked into a slow, easy smile that answered my question before he'd even opened his mouth. "A lil' bit," he admitted. "Had an early shift at the shop, then was there *all fuckin day*," he groaned. "So... yeah. I may have done something to take the edge off."

"I didn't know *edge* was even possible with you. You're so laid back," I said.

He shrugged. "Everybody has their shit, you know?"

"I don't, actually." I raised an eyebrow at him. "I don't know much about you at all."

"I could say the same, so what are we going to do to fix that?"

"What makes you think it's something to be fixed?"

"Because I say it is. That's enough, right?" he asked, with a fresh grin that made me... squirm a little in my seat.

I didn't like how much I liked the way he made me feel.

Very suddenly, the others started up a round of loud whistles and cheers, with Tristan joining in. I followed their attention to the stage, where a man and woman who were obvious crowd favorites had stepped forward.

"That's Eddie," Tristan explained, answering the question that must've been apparent on my face. "He owns the tattoo shop. Astrid is his lady, she owns the yoga studio."

Yeah.

Looking at them, it tracked.

"What are they about to do?" I asked, unable to pull my eyes away from them. They were both beautiful.

"Eddie draws, Astrid does poetry. It's good stuff."

Any further explanation he may have planned to offer, was cut short by music. On the stage, Eddie and Astrid had finished their set up, with Astrid stepping up to the mic amid applause to say, "This... is *Reinvention*."

Just the mention of that word I'd claimed for myself had me sitting straight up in my seat, attention rapt as they began. My gaze followed every stroke of Eddie's thick charcoal pencil, my ears keenly tuned to Astrid's words as she spoke the process of rebirthing yourself, and what it required.

The energy.

The healing.

The focus.

The willingness to fuck it all up and simply try again.

And again.

The courage to stop thinking about it, and actually *do it*.

It was overwhelming.

But I couldn't tune it out.

I watched Eddie draw the beautifully detailed phoenix while Astrid spoke of pulling herself, beautiful and whole, from the ashes of what she once was.

I had to fight back tears.

The absolute last thing I was about to do was cry in a crowded room of strangers about a poem, but my hold on that particular resolve was tenuous at best. Especially when, after their performance, Eddie and Astrid came by the table to say hello.

She took one look at me, sitting there by myself because I didn't know them to be jumping up to offer hugs. So she came to me instead, arms outstretched, and I returned the gesture because I didn't want to be – more – weird.

But then, she put her mouth right next to my ear, and said, "You're going to be okay."

I wanted to ask what the hell that meant but she'd already moved on, speaking to someone else. In "typical" circumstances, I might've snatched her up, forcing an explanation out of her, but for now I had to swallow that urge.

"You good?" Tristan asked, his big hands closing over my arms as he bent to look me in the face. "You look spooked."

I glanced to where Astrid was, still confused as hell by what had just happened.

"*Ohhh*," Tristan groaned. "She say something to you?"

My eyebrows shot up. "Yeah."

"She swears she's not a psychic, but man... she knows stuff. It wasn't anything bad, was it?"

I blinked. "No. No, not at all."

"Okay then... come to the bar with me. Let's drink to whatever she told you."

You're going to be okay.

Yeah.

I... guess that *was* something to drink to.

So we did.

Multiple times.

I didn't take it far enough to get drunk, but I was *certainly* feeling much more mellow than when I arrived by the time Tristan decided we needed more privacy than the large booth with the group allowed.

Even with the liquor in my system, I was grateful for the much quieter corner he found.

And... I was actually having a good time.

After Eddie and Astrid, there was a comedian who'd come on, a singer after that, and then a whole band. Every act was *really* talented.

At some point, I realized Tristan had completely abandoned any pretense of watching the stage to watch me instead. I ignored it at first, but after the next performer left the stage, I turned to him, arms crossed.

"Whatever you're about to say, know that your annoyance makes you even finer," he said, before I could even open my mouth. And just that quickly, I was laughing instead of scolding him. "Damn, I was wrong," he grinned, biting his lip. "The smile..."

I shook my head, forcing my face into a neutral expression. "Mmmhmm. Here I was thinking you'd sobered up some, but you are definitely still... lifted."

"You don't think you have a pretty smile?"

"I *know* I do. I also know I'm *much* finer when I'm mad."

Tristan chuckled, leaning toward me so our shoulders were touching. "Okay. Maybe the smile hits me in a different place then, how about that?"

"I wouldn't know," I told him, then glanced at the time on his watch face. "Shouldn't you be tucking in your kid or something, instead of out... caking?"

His eyebrows went up. "Caking?"

"Yes, *caking*," I repeated. "Or what, do people not call it that anymore?"

"I wouldn't know," he shrugged. "And my kid is with her mom tonight, so she's good."

"Is that why you were stressed out enough earlier to need to..." I made a smoking gesture with my fingers, and he laughed.

"Nah, nothing to do with that. The drama stays at a minimum."

"With the kid, or the mother?"

"Both," he chuckled. "Kiara and Von, they're laid back."

I nodded. "Nice. A whole little laid-back family."

"Ah, *hell*," he groaned. "Here you go…"

"Here I go? What am I doing?"

"Making it seem like it's something it isn't."

"Okay so tell me what it is then."

He sat up, looking me right in the face. "I'm Tristan Grimes. When I was sixteen years old, I met Yvonne, who I thought was the love of my life. When we were seventeen, we fucked up, had a kid. I didn't have shit else going for me, so as soon as I was old enough, I joined the military as a means to take care of my little instant family. To that end… it worked out, I guess. Me and Yvonne did not – we don't fit together romantically as adults, but that's my homie. We do not still fuck around when we get bored, damn," he chuckled.

"I didn't even say anything!" I insisted, which only made him laugh harder.

"It was all over your face, as soon as I said *homie*."

Fine.

Maybe it was.

"I know you have no reason to believe that shit, especially since you *just* found out I even had a kid, but… you asked what it was, and that's it. You're interested in me, and I'm interested in you. That's it."

"Do you think if you repeat that enough times, it'll be true?"

He sucked his teeth. "Temp, stop playing."

"Stop calling me *Temp*."

"Do you not like *that* nickname, or no nicknames period?"

"I didn't say I didn't like it," I countered. "I said stop saying it."

"Why?"

"Because nicknames are for... lovers, and friends, and family, and hell... people who *actually* know each other. And as we've established, I don't know you. You don't know me."

"Right, and that's an error I'm doing my damndest to correct, if you'd stop trying to cut me off at the knees. What's so wrong with some mutual interest between us?" he asked, his handsome face pulled into an attentive scowl as he waited for an answer I didn't have.

"I should go."

I said that, but didn't move until Tristan nodded. "Let me walk you."

Once again, I found myself grateful for the hint of coolness in the air – it was what I needed to dampen all the inconvenient feelings this night had ignited. Between that fucking poem, the drinks, and Tristan's undivided attention, my face was hot and my mind was reeling, and I truly wasn't sure what to do with myself.

I had no idea what I was doing.

At *all*.

"Please tell me you at least had a better time tonight than when ol' boy put his hands on you?" Tristan asked, speaking for the first time since we stepped outside. The walk across the street had been quiet, which I didn't mind.

I was still trying to figure this all out.

"What do you mean *at least*? Do I seem like I had a bad time?"

"Well, considering the way you were suddenly ready to go, I thought I'd said the wrong thing or something."

I let out a sigh, pressing my back to the little inset frame of the candle shop door. "The *wrong thing* is pretty subjective."

"So what I said was fine, you just weren't trying to hear it?"

he asked, leaning against the opposite side, facing me. "I mean, that's what I'm hearing."

"Maybe," I admitted. "Or... maybe I'm tired. I didn't get much sleep last night."

"Me either," Tristan nodded. "So we've got something in common."

I huffed. "Somehow, I doubt our reasons for not being able to sleep are the same."

"Yeah," he agreed. "I doubt you dream about covert orders and combat situations. Well... I guess they wouldn't be dreams, really. More like nightmares."

I met his gaze for a moment, shocked, before it clicked for me that he was talking about himself. As much as I wanted to tell him that yes, actually, I definitely had nightmares about those *exact* things... I knew I couldn't.

Or... *shouldn't.*

"So that's what you were so stressed about?"

He blinked.

Then nodded.

"Yeah," he confirmed, with a deep sigh like he was embarrassed to admit it. "It's... something I struggle with, a little bit."

"A little bit, or a lot?"

A dry laugh wrangled from his throat as he pushed a handful of locs back from his face, meeting my gaze again. "A lot."

"Me too."

"Hopefully tonight will be better for both of us," he replied, with zero innuendo in his tone.

My brain took it there, immediately thinking of a way we could end this night with a definite bang, and go ahead and rid the air between us of the pesky sexual tension.

"Do you want to come inside?"

His eyebrows went up, obviously surprised that I'd asked – and hell, I was kinda surprised myself. We'd exchanged nothing more intimate than a hug, but here I was, basically offering him pussy? What the hell was I thi—

"I probably shouldn't."

Oh.

I'd, eventually, have figured out how to rationalize having sex with a near stranger – it wasn't as if that was far-fetched for me, especially considering some of the things I'd done in the name of a completing a mission.

What threatened to break me, was this firm rejection, when I'd thought – when *he* made it seem like – he wanted me.

Badly.

Shit.

"Of course," I stammered, pushing out an awkward laugh. "I shouldn't assume you want to fuck me just because you've... been in my face, nonstop, acting like you want to fuck me."

"Temp, it's not—"

"*Stop calling me that,*" I snapped, suddenly back on the verge of tears I'd overridden three times in the last twenty-four hours already. I was out of practice now – I wasn't sure I could keep holding them back. "And you don't have to try to spare my feelings – you can go."

"It ain't *that* either," he countered, pushing off from the wall to get in my face.

"What is it then?"

"*This.*"

The *this* he spoke of was an arm around my waist, pulling me against him, and a hand in my hair, fingers tangled in the strands as his mouth came to mine.

His soft full lips against mine, his tongue in my mouth, his hardness pressed against my stomach, his hand sliding from my waist to grip my ass as he deepened the kiss...

I felt it everywhere.

The giddy lightheadedness, the flutters deep in my belly, the throbbing heat between my legs...

This was... everything.

And it was over much too soon.

"I don't want to come inside tonight, because... I like you. And I would like it to just... be that, before we make it something else," he murmured against my lips before he finally pulled back.

"You don't know me."

He smirked. "And I've already explained how I feel about that. So..."

"So, what?" I asked, my heart still racing from the sudden excitement of that kiss.

"So... stop fucking around Temp...*est,*" he quickly added, with a goofy grin that I couldn't help responding to in kind. "Meaning... let me get to know you."

"I don't want to." I shook my head. "Getting to know people is... messy. And hard. Coming upstairs is very, *very* easy."

Tristan drug his teeth over his lip, nodding. "Yeah. That's exactly why I'm not interested in that, sweetheart. Goodnight," he said, pulling me close again without any type of warning, for another kiss.

A quick one this time, but with the same type of butterflies.

I... didn't know what to say.

So instead of trying, I said nothing, just returned his wave when he started to walk off.

"Go inside, T, so I know you got *all the way* home safe," he called to me before he turned to make sure I was doing so.

Instead, he caught me staring after him.

Embarrassed, I quickly retrieved my keys, not even looking back until I was on the other side of the door.

He waved again, and I waved back, then rushed upstairs to see the street so I could watch him walk past.

Like some silly girl with a crush.

Which... I guess was pretty damn accurate.

chapter six

THE MORE I THOUGHT ABOUT HIM DECLINING MY INVITATION, THE angrier I got.

Being turned down was not... a thing that happened to me.

Granted, every sexual experience I could remember had been very specifically targeted – the way I looked, the things I'd said, the clothes I'd worn... everything was curated and neatly typed out along with a slew of other information telling me exactly what my mark wanted.

Tristan wasn't a mark though.

And what he wanted wasn't... *me*.

He kissed you though.

And explained exactly why he didn't want to have sex yet.

Sure.

Logically, I understood the contradiction.

But, I was no longer operating on pure logic and calculated steps – it *felt* really shitty, that my first attempt at intimacy with someone who wasn't part of a mission had been a fucking failure.

Because it wasn't just a thing that happened – not for someone like me.

Failure was a complete state of being, a disappointment that deserved to be punished, harshly.

And hell... it was *confusing*.

A *man*.

Not fucking someone he supposedly liked.

Men would fuck people they *didn't* like, at peril of losing their family, friends, jobs, whole livelihoods.

Hell.

Their *lives*.

It's bullshit. Maybe you're not his type.

No, *that* was bullshit.

I was everybody's fucking *type*.

I kept my honey-toned skin glowing and flawless, kept my body fat punished into submission, hair nourished and healthy, and I couldn't take any credit for my face, but that was fucking amazing too.

There was nothing wrong with *me*.

There was something wrong with *him*.

Yeah, yeah, you're cute.

*But seriously, could you be **any** weirder?*

Oh.

Yeah.

There *was* that, huh?

I hadn't exactly been at my most charming, hadn't yet mastered the keeping of my cool around Tristan yet. I always felt so brutally awkward, that it only made sense for him to have picked up on the same thing.

He kissed you though.

Yes.

He did.

And what a kiss it had been.

Essentially my *first*, at least on a personal level.

Problem was, I hadn't seen or heard from him in the several days passed since then.

Had I left my house and been in public?

No.

Did he have my number?

Also no.

Had I answered the bell at the candle shop for anyone?

Still no.

But *still.*

If he was really interested, he wouldn't let silly things like that stop him, so I *had* to assume this was all something for me to take as a lesson and move on.

All the shit I'd ordered for the shop was due to arrive today.

In fact, only a few moments after the thought crossed my mind, I watched a delivery truck pull up, causing a spark of excitement to bloom in my chest.

Which made me even happier.

Excitement was good.

I rushed downstairs, making it to the door before the delivery person had even touched the bell. Hurriedly, I signed the little electronic clipboard to confirm it was me, then stepped aside so my packages could be brought inside.

As soon as they were gone, I dived right in.

I took my time with the unpacking, making sure to put everything in the spots I'd already planned out back in the workroom. Never mind that I *really* didn't quite know what I was doing – I was looking forward to the prospect of figuring it all out.

"Wow. You're getting a whole business set up back here, huh?"

The box of wooden wicks I was holding dropped from my hands, my head whipping around for the source of those words.

Tristan.

"How did you get in here?" I asked, swallowing hard.

Damn he looked good this morning, in navy sweats and a matching tee, freshly retwisted locs, neatly groomed beard.

"The door was open..." he said, gesturing behind him. "I figured you were letting some fresh air in or something."

"So you took that as an invitation?" I brushed past him to get to the front door, where it was indeed *wide open* from where I'd propped it for the boxes to be brought in.

"Yes, actually." When I turned from closing the door, he was *right* behind me, smelling like fresh laundry and cedar, and... pissing me off. "You haven't exactly been accessible, so I took the opportunity that presented itself."

I took a step back, trying to breathe in something that wasn't *him*. "So this is my fault?"

"Fault?" He raised a thick eyebrow at me, and frowned. "*Fault* implies that something is wrong. Is something wrong between us?"

"*Us?*" I propped my hands on my hips. "*Us* implies that such a thing exists."

He stared at me for a long moment before a slow smirk spread across his lips. "You're upset about me not coming upstairs with you the other night."

"What? *No!*" I snapped. "Why would I be pressed about that? I could have any man I wanted around here, and you think I'm hung up on you not wanting to fuck me?"

You definitely are ...

"It's *exactly* what I think," he scoffed. "You are *absolutely* tripping on that shit, and I... don't understand why. It's a problem for me to want to know you better before being intimate?"

"The intimacy will better inform if I *want* to know you," I countered, not backing down even though I could feel myself digging deeper into an even worse space than we already were.

"I guess we're at an impasse then?"

I shrugged. "I guess so. Can you leave now?"

"No, I'm not fucking *leaving*," he grunted, throwing up his hands. "I'm trying to bluff your stubborn ass into... shit, I don't even know. You're frustrating the hell outta me right now – I thought women *liked* when niggas weren't trying to jump straight into bed."

"I'm not this nebulous *women* you speak of – I'm Tempest," I told him. "I can't speak for what anyone else likes, but no, *I* didn't like offering myself to you and getting turned down. It didn't feel good. At all."

He pushed out a sigh. "I get that. And I'm sorry for making you feel bad – that wasn't my intention at all. It had nothing to do with me not finding you attractive, or anything like that. I thought I'd made myself clear."

"You *did* make yourself clear, as far as I'm concerned."

His expression shifted back to a smile. "So we're good then?"

I returned his smile. "You're good. I'm good. And you can go now."

"Wait, what?"

"You heard exactly what I said," I told him, pulling the door open and gesturing for him to step out.

Was I making a mistake here?

Probably.

Would I regret it?

Probably.

Could I let go of my stubbornness long enough to accept his words, instead of my perception, as the truth, and move forward from there?

Absolutely not.

He let out another heavy sigh before he stepped out, turning to say something as soon as he was on the other side of my threshold.

I wasn't trying to hear it.

I closed and locked the door, then moved back to my workshop, leaving him standing there looking dumbfounded.

Good.

I hoped he felt as confused as I had.

I COULDN'T LET IT GO.

Which is what a person who *really* wasn't bothered would've done.

Nope.

Instead of minding my business and making some damn candles, I found myself at *Urban Grind,* in skintight jeans, a lowcut top and no bra, heels, hair and makeup done to perfection.

Seeking attention.

When Tristan was very clearly at work.

Just like the first night I met him, he had on the *security* tee shirt, helping keep the weekend crowd under control. And just like any other time we were in the same room, he spotted me.

Only now, I didn't quite feel like I could trust what I'd *thought* was obvious attraction in his eyes.

I could, however, trust these other motherfuckers.

They weren't shy at all with their intentions, and I believed them when it all came spilling from their mouths, fueled by liquor and marijuana and my blatant flirting. After that confusing ass encounter with Tristan, the brazen attempts to take me home – or to the bathroom – were actually... kinda soothing.

I *hadn't* lost my touch.

"We really should get out of here, you know..."

I couldn't remember his name, but he really *did* look good. Tall and sandy, slim and well-dressed, and very, *very* pretty.

And his breath smelled good.

"Let me guess... you wanna get to know me better?" I practically purred, pressing myself into his chest as he curled an arm around my waist... with Tristan looking on.

I could feel his annoyance from across the room.

Whatever-his-name-was grinned at me, the metallic glint of his grill flashing before he dipped his head to speak into my ear. "Certain places on you? Absolutely?"

I giggled about that – his words, and the minty-coolness of his breath against my skin. Biting my lip, I stared up at him, and was damn near ready to ask where we were going when he suddenly snatched away from me.

Or, more accurately, when Tristan snatched him away from me.

"What is the problem?" he yelped, glowering as Tristan got in his face.

"You tell me, bruh," Tristan growled, wearing this terrifyingly cold expression that sent a chill up my spine... and between my legs.

My potential dick for the night took a step back, hands up. "That's you?" he asked, pointing to me.

"No!" I answered, at the same time that Tristan said "*Sure is.*"

Obviously, that eliminated any "potential".

"What the *fuck*?" I asked Tristan, ignoring the eyes that had been drawn by that little scene to confront him. "Why would you do that?"

"Why would *you*?" he countered.

"Because I'm a grown ass woman, and I can do what I want – and what I *want* is hot, meaningless sex," I told him. "So unless you're planning to offer that – stay out of my way."

Tristan's nostrils flared as he stared at me, clearly trying to gather his words.

He was taking too damn long.

I started to walk away, only to have him grab me by the arm, pulling me through the crowd to the back hallways of the coffeehouse, where I snatched away from him.

"*Why* are you playing with me?" he asked, before I could start cursing him out for grabbing me.

"Nobody is playing with you. This isn't even *about* you," I lied. "But I guess being the neighborhood hottie doesn't come without a healthy dose of narcissism, huh?"

"So you're *not* in here looking good as fuck in these other niggas faces, to make me jealous?"

I grinned. "... you think I look good?"

"*Obviously.*"

"Nope," I shook my head. "If it was so *obvious*, you'd have come upstairs the other night and given me what *I* needed. And since you won't – I'll find someone who *will*."

I turned to walk away, only to have him grab me again, sandwiching me between his body and the wall.

"No, you won't," he told me, like it was up to him.

"*Fuck you.*"

Tristan smirked, bringing his mouth *almost* to mine as he tightened his grip on my wrists. "Is that what I have to do, huh? Fuck some cooperation into you?"

"Yes. Please," I murmured, making him chuckle as our lips pressed together. I pulled my wrists from his hold to fist handfuls of his shirt instead, pulling him into me as his tongue slipped into my mouth.

Devouring me.

He palmed my ass, easily lifting me to press into the wall behind us as my legs hiked around his waist. His dick was hard, and thick, pushing against the space between my legs – not *remotely* helping my soaked-panty situation.

Tristan's mouth dropped to my neck, sucking, licking, biting, kissing, driving me crazy. He slid a hand between us, easily finding the spot, even through the thin barrier of my jeans, that had me panting as soon as he touched me there.

He didn't just touch though.

He pressed, and rubbed, creating an inexcusably pleasurable friction that had me whimpering into his mouth as he kissed me.

"You want me to make you cum?" he asked, pulling away from my mouth to graze my earlobe with his teeth.

"*Yes*," I answered, breathlessly.

"You're gonna stop the games?"

"What games?"

His hand came away, and I quickly grabbed his wrist, bringing it back.

"Yes," I told him. "But..."

"But what?" he murmured, doing something to my ear with his tongue that almost made me cum right then, with his fingers pressed to my clit through my jeans.

"I... *need this*," I whimpered, telling the truth even though it was weak as hell to admit.

"You need... to cum?"

I nodded, offering an assenting groan into his mouth as he kissed me again, and finally started again with the friction from his fingers.

And this was blissful, really.

But no... this wasn't what I needed.

I needed more – needed the experience, needed everything. No, I wasn't a virgin, but now I needed my own, *personal* experiences to replace the mission-critical ones that had shaped me.

I needed something else in my head.

Something I'd chosen, something that was *mine*.

And no, of course, I didn't *want* that to be with some random – especially not with these budding feelings I was having for Tristan.

But I also didn't want to "wait".

Couldn't wait, now that I had it in my head.

This was a start, but I needed... *more*.

Wanted more.

Wanted... *him*.

The orgasm hit me *very* suddenly, the physiological response ripping me out of my thoughts and firmly into the moment.

The tensing of my whole body, the rush of sensation, the feeling of euphoria.

Tristan swallowing my exaltations of pleasure in a kiss.

My breath happened in soft pants as I came down from the orgasmic high, with Tristan keeping me steady as I found balance on the floor in my heels.

For a long moment, we couldn't do anything but look at each other.

And then...

"Give me your number."

I raised an eyebrow. "What?"

"Your *number*," he repeated. "You know, the specific-to-you series of digits that allows people to call or message the little device you carry around."

"You're not funny. Or cute."

He scoffed. "I see a lie *still* don't care who tells it, huh?"

He pulled his phone from his pocket, unlocking the screen before he put it in my hand, then gestured for mine.

So... I gave it to him.

And I put the correct number in his, too.

"You got a text," I told him, returning the phone and taking mine back. "Somebody asking where you are. You're probably about to get fired."

"This is mostly a favor anyway," he countered. "One of the regular security guys is out for a few weeks, they needed somebody to fill in. Kiara wants new clothes, so I could use the extra bread to offset to my bank account. Everybody's happy."

"Except whoever might be getting their ribs kicked in because *security* is busy finger-popping a woman who wants dick."

He smirked. "Technically, finger-popping would require penetration, but I get your point."

"You definitely get my point."

"And I made you cum. *Hard.*"

I let out a dry laugh, shifting in my ruined panties over the reminder. "You did. And yet..."

"You'll get your dick, damn, woman," he fussed. "I'm just... trying to do something different here. Something... healthy. If you'll work with me, please?"

And what about what I'm trying to do?

I thought it, but didn't say it out loud, because honestly... now that I was in some kinda post-orgasm high... the sound of it kinda appealed to me too.

And Alicia would be proud.

Probably.

"Just get back to what you're supposed to be doing," I said, shrugging it off.

"Does that mean you're taking your fine ass home? *Alone?*"

"You're really pressed about that, aren't you?"

"I really fucking am," he admitted. "Like... I was about to whoop ol' boy's ass."

I smirked. "Well... you can keep your hands to yourself over me tonight," I told him, even though... I kinda liked that energy.

Really liked it.

Which was probably not good, but whatever.

"You sure?" he asked, putting his hands at my waist to pull me against him.

"Yeah," I nodded, then accepted the soft, quick kiss he offered. "I'm going home. *Alone.*"

So... I did exactly that, after we'd said our goodbyes.

I showered, and got into bed, and then, before I drifted off, when Tristan's name flashed on my screen with a text... I smiled.

Maybe something really was going right?

chapter seven

"Go for a walk with me. – Neighborhood Hottie"

The already quite pleasing occurrence of Tristan texting was somehow even better now that I'd changed his name in my phone – the whole *neighborhood hottie* thing was quite amusing to me.

What was *not* amusing was this text coming through at five-something in the morning, breaking into my tenuous hold on the fringes of a good night's sleep.

"A walk? What are you even talking about?" I texted back, planting my face in the pillow after I'd dropped the phone back down on the bed. A moment later, it buzzed again, with a message that despite my annoyance, made me laugh.

"Yes, a walk. You know... that thing you do with your feet, to get around? – Neighborhood Hottie"

"Kiss my ass."

"You'd enjoy that way too much. – Neighborhood Hottie."

I groaned, and stuck my face right back into the pillow to scream, because... yes.

Yes I would.

I was so fucking *weak.*

So... *horny.*

Like nothing I'd ever, *ever* experienced before.

That little bit of relief Tristan had given me at the coffeehouse that night had lasted all of maybe an hour before I was right back to thinking about how I could make him give me what I wanted.

And I could, definitely, *make him* give me what I wanted.

If only these pesky ass feelings weren't in the way.

"So... you coming or not? I'll be at your door in five minutes. – Neighborhood Hottie"

Wait.

What?!

I sprung out of bed, racing to the bathroom to brush my teeth and wash my face. Luckily, my silk scarf had stayed put last night, which made it easy to brush my hair into a simple ponytail.

I never did make it back to the phone in time to respond to that text – in exactly the five minutes he'd mentioned, the bell at the candle shop door rang, while I was still getting dressed.

Shit.

I jogged down the stairs in bike shorts and a sports bra, figuring I could at least make him look at what he was choosing not to have.

He didn't disappoint.

The look on his face – the *lust* in his eyes – was quite gratifying when I opened the door to him holding two cups from *Urban Grind.*

"Good morning," he said, clearing his throat before forcing his gaze to remain at my face. "I brought you that tea thing that you like."

"Thank you." I accepted the cup, and gestured for him to step inside. "And good morning to you too. I just... I was asleep when you texted, so I need a few more minutes to finish up. If you wanna come upstairs. You can keep your pants on, I promise."

*Why the fuck did you say **that**?*

"Uh... yeah. I can come up there," he replied. "Only since you promised."

I'd already started up the stairs, but looked back, smirking when I realized his eyes were glued to my ass as he followed me up. "There's plenty of things that don't require your pants coming off, Tristan."

"Could you not?" he groaned, and I laughed as I finished climbing the last few steps. I pushed my door open and went inside, searching out socks, shoes, and a tee shirt to complete my outfit for this...

"Is this a date?" I asked, peeking around the partition I'd put up as a bedroom "wall". I couldn't be sure he actually heard me – he was too busy looking around in awe.

"So this is your space, huh?" he asked, the wonderment on his face being taken over by a smile. "It's... bright."

I took a sip from the drink he'd brought – a *mocha matcha madness* – then raised an eyebrow. "Why do you seem so surprised by that?"

"It's ... not what I expected," he said, stepping over to the window to look out. "I mean, you had me tattoo a storm on you, and you're all on your mystery shit... I thought your space would be moody or something. This is ... *pretty*."

Once I'd pulled my shirt over my head, I looked around, trying to see what he saw. And... yeah, I guess I did. My chosen color palette involved lots of whites and delicate grays, with the occasional pale touch of teal. Lots of soft textures to break up the hard surfaces, no darkness.

I wanted a space that made me feel good, and... this did.

When I told him that, his lips spread into a full-blown smile. "Thank you for inviting me into your sanctuary."

I shrugged. "Thank my mentor. She's the one who encouraged me to be more trusting, and open, so..."

"A mentor? That's dope," Tristan nodded, following me back to the door now that I had on shoes and had grabbed my latte, keys, and everything for my little crossbody pouch. "It's nice to have that guidance and all that."

"Yeah. She um... used to be in the same industry as me, so she kinda understands all the... unique challenges of transitioning out of it. She's really been a life saver for me."

"Ay – you never did tell me what you used to do," he spoke up, as we stepped out of the shop. "Did I tell you Kiara thinks you're a spy?"

I smiled. "I thought it was an assassin. At least, that's what she said to *me*."

"It's evolved to both," he explained, chuckling. "I suppose I shouldn't complain about the girl having an imagination, right?"

"Let her dream." I took a sip from my drink, enjoying the kick of warmth against the cool spring morning – the sun wasn't quite up yet, so my shorts and tee shirt weren't quite doing the trick. "I'm not offended."

"Hm... is that because you *are* a spy?"

"It's because I understand that kids are kids, and *should* be free to make decisions, and have their own minds. She wasn't timid, or afraid to say what she was thinking – which I think says a lot about you, as her parent. So... I guess... good job."

Tristan grinned. "Well thank you... but you do realize you didn't actually deny being a spy, right?" he laughed. "Why are you being so cagey about this job thing? You used to run drugs or something? Cause there's plenty of folks like that around here, nothing to be embarrassed about. Hell, I introduced you to *several* felons that night I invited you to *Urban Grind*."

My eyes went wide. "Duly noted. And I hear you, I get where you're coming from, but... I really *don't* want to talk about my job. *Won't* talk about it. It was pretty traumatizing, and ... something I want to move past, completely." I stopped walking. "I get it, if you're not willing to accept that. We can turn back now, and drop this here."

He sucked his teeth, shifting the hand he was holding his cup with to grab mine, pulling me to get me walking again. "I thought I told you to stop playing with me?"

"What?"

"If there's shit you don't want to talk about, we don't have to talk about it. But you're loco if you think something like that is gonna scare me off easily. You can cross that one off your list of excuses – from now on, you're the candle lady to me. Far as I'm concerned, making candles is the only thing you've *ever* done."

"Only, I haven't even made *one* candle. Ever," I corrected him, information he met with a frown.

"I watched you get a whole shipment of shit last week, and you were looking around at it all like a kid in a candy store."

"Yeah," I admitted. "I *was* excited to get it, but now that it's all here, I... I dunno. It's kinda intimidating."

Immediately, Tristan frowned, brushing off my words. "Man, whatever."

"What?"

"I don't believe for a second that you're intimidated by... anything, honestly," he said, stopping with me at an intersection. I met his gaze, thinking he had to be joking, because... seriously?

Every element of this whole *reinvention* thing was intimidating as fuck.

There was no way with as much as I felt it, he couldn't see how confused and awkward I was. Especially with *him*.

"I'm glad you think so highly of me," I told him as we crossed the street. "But I'm really feeling my way through the dark. I'm really not used to being able to make my own decisions, and just... living exactly how I want. Yes, I've lived, and all that, but now that it's all just up to me... it's so different. Everything is brand new, all over."

"Damn," Tristan nodded. "That's... intense. I get it though. Well, kinda. I was deployed, you know? *Kept* getting sent back. And when you're out in all these foreign places, enmeshed in real fucking combat, conflicts that "regular" people don't even know about... it's like, you come back to a whole different world. And it's not that you can't function, because you can, but it's so damn... *different*."

I thought he would say more – *wanted* him to say more – but instead, he trailed off. He was talking about his own, very separate experience, but everything he'd said, I'd absolutely been feeling.

He was right.

It wasn't that you couldn't function, it was so damn... *different*.

"It sounds like you've seen a lot," I said, prompting him to break away from whatever was happening in his head that had him staring off in the distance, to nod.

"Yeah. Too much for my years." He took a sip from his cup, then smirked at me. "I swear I'm not trying to pry about your last job that didn't exist, but... I feel like you probably can relate to that."

"To what? Having seen too much?"

He nodded.

"Oh," I laughed. "You have no idea."

"Yeah I thought so," he replied. "Hey, how old are you?"

My eyes went wide. "How old am I?"

"Yes. As in, when is your birthday?"

"Oh. I... uh—"

I was saved from that question – one I had no real answer for – by a sudden blaring of music, which I quickly realized was coming from the pocket of Tristan's basketball shorts.

"*Boyz II Men*?" I asked, wrinkling my nose. "*Seriously*?"

He offered an embarrassed grin as he shrugged, retrieving his phone. "It's my mother. She picked it," he explained, his thumb hovering over the screen. "Hold on," he said to me, then tapped the screen and lifted it to his here. "Good morning beautiful," he greeted, which made me have to bite back a smile. "I'm a little occupied right now, can I call you back? I – no, I do not think you're one of the regular women out here," he said, putting a hand to his face. "No, I never doubted you, I said I didn't *believe* – I... okay. Okay. Okay. I'm sorry. I love you."

"Well... that was a really interesting conversation, from *this* end at least," I said, watching as, instead of putting his phone away, he tapped a few more times on the screen.

"Because my mother is a complete mess," he explained, holding up his phone to show me a picture on the screen, of a beautiful older black woman holding a large bouquet of flowers. She was wearing a tee shirt with "*Unfuckwittable*" printed across the front, and a facial expression that said... the same thing, honestly.

"I feel like this requires an explanation," I said, meeting his gaze, which was brimming with amusement.

He chuckled as he slipped it back in his pocket. "Well, you know Mother's Day was a couple weeks ago, right? Well, she loves getting flowers, so that's what I did. I made a comment to her about not being sad when they wilted or whatever, since that's what always happens to cut flowers, but she was like... nah, I'ma keep my shit alive. So I told her, mama, I don't think it works like that. I believe you can keep them two weeks tops, at *max*. So... basically she took it as a personal challenge, cause this is week three, and they still look really good. She was calling to rub it in my face."

"*Wow*," I laughed, when he finished. "Your mother sounds... amazing, to be frank."

"You know... I would agree with that," he nodded. "She's always been good at bringing stuff back to life, keeping it alive. I don't think we ever had a pet growing up that wasn't half-dead when we got it, then thriving by the time she was through with it. She has this energy about her."

"I feel like I could tell that from the picture. Like she's really warm, and sweet, but also not to be played with."

"And you would be exactly right," he laughed. "Love that lady, man. What about you?" he asked, after we'd gone a little further, in silence. "What's your mother like?"

"Oh! Um... I don't know, actually."

The smile he'd been wearing dissolved. "Shit. My bad. Were you... adopted?"

"Something like that," I said, nodding. "I don't have any family, nothing like that. So, besides my mentor and few others, I don't... I don't really have anyone."

We walked in silence for a few *more* moments, and then... "That's fucked up."

"Yeah," I agreed, with a dry laugh. "It is."

"But you can't say it anymore."

I raised an eyebrow at him. "Excuse me?"

"You can't claim to not have anybody anymore, because *now*... you've got *me*. And I'm worth at least ten motherfuckers," he said, barely keeping a straight face for that last part, which made it impossible for me not to laugh too.

"Ay, I'm serious," he said, after a few seconds had passed. "I know we're still kinda feeling each other out, but if you need anything... you've got my number. And if you *want* anything... my number works for that, too."

He was looking me right in the face when he said that, holding my gaze so there was no downplaying the significance of his words. It was a little overwhelming – so much that I broke into a smile, because I didn't know what else to do, and was about to crack a joke about sex to break the tension when someone else called out.

"*Tristaaaan!*"

He and I both turned in the direction of the voice, to see a woman practically running up the street toward us. When I looked at Tristan, he was smiling, which... annoyed me.

"*Nya!*" he greeted her with a laugh. "How you doing baby?"

Baby?

Once she was actually close to us, they hugged – too tight, and too long.

I didn't like it.

And I *hated* it when, afterward, she kept her arm draped around his waist, and a hand at his chest, like they were taking fucking engagement pictures or something.

Should I kill her?

"Who is this?" she asked, her silky, sandy-brown hair bouncing around her shoulders to frame her face in perfect layers as her head whipped in my direction. Her tone was light, but she didn't even bother hiding the disdain in her hazel eyes, since Tristan couldn't see her face.

Yeah. I should.

"This is Tempest," Tristan spoke, easing from her hold to step to my side, placing a possessive hand at the small of my back. "We were out for a walk."

"Like a date? This early?" she laughed. "You must be getting this one out of the way for when we get together later."

Definitely gonna kill this bitch.

"You wild, Nya," he said, shifting that hand to wrap his arm around my shoulders instead, like he could hear my thoughts and was trying to keep me still. "We're walking over to the park, to see the sun rise over the lake."

"*Awww.* How romantic," she gushed.

Fake.

"I thought so too. I thought you might like it," he said, to me, and I forced a smile as I looked up at him.

Not because he was wrong.

Because it was taking a lot for me to not leave my murderous desires on my face.

"You thought right," I told him, and was rewarded for my cooperation with a soft press of his lips.

"All this sweetness is going to make me throw up," Nya laughed.

Again – fake.

"I can't believe you're giving all this bae behavior to someone else, Tris – you were supposed to wait for me," she pouted, blinking at him with her freakishly long lash extensions.

"You snooze, you lose," was his only response to that. "We've gotta get on if we don't want to miss this timing," he said, already starting to move again, and pulling me along with him.

"Okay lovebirds," she trilled. "I've gotta get to the salon anyway. I'll see *you* later."

That inflection she put on *you* had me ready to show Tristan that his arm around me wasn't holding a single thing back – I didn't want to show my ass about something so small.

"Former girlfriend," Tristan said, apparently understanding the importance of being proactive. "*Far* former. Like years ago, former."

"Seems like she still wants you."

"Because she saw you – Nya enjoys drama, which is why she's a *former* girlfriend. Let's talk about something important."

I laughed. "Okay... such as?"

"Such as you not knowing when your birthday is," he answered. "Is it because of the adoption? Records lost or something?"

"Yeah."

Sure.

We could call it that.

"You know, you should talk to Troy – he has experience with that, and doing the ancestry tests and stuff. He actually found out he had a whole twin brother," Tristan said. "It might be good to chop it up with somebody who's been through it. Maybe?"

I nodded. "Maybe. I... am probably not gonna do that, though."

"Yeah I knew it was a long shot when I said it," he laughed. "I wanted to at least try."

"I appreciate that. Um... about this sunrise thing..."

I'd actually never been this far down the main street, and had no idea it ended in a park – especially not one as big as what we'd walked up on. It was beautifully spread out, with a decent-sized lake and dock, with people already out with their fishing rods and other gear.

Even a few small boats.

"I hope that's not *too* corny for you, is it?" he asked.

I shook my head. "No. Not at all."

We found a small bench and sat down together – closer than necessary. Despite *Nya* and her interruption, we'd made it right on time.

And it was... beautiful.

"I come out here when I can't get back to sleep. It feels peaceful, you know?"

"Yeah, it is," I agreed. "That's what happened to you this morning? You couldn't sleep?"

He nodded. "I was on my way here, stopped at *UG*, looked across the street... thought it would be nice to have some company."

"So you thought since you couldn't sleep, I shouldn't either?"

Tristan pulled his gaze away from the view to grin at me. "Yes. *Exactly*. Thank you for understanding."

"*Asshole*," I laughed, nudging his shoulder with mine until he gave in and laughed too. After a moment, he put his arm around my shoulders again, pulling me into him, and... I couldn't help it.

I dropped my head against him, and let myself be comfortable with being so damned comfortable.

"Thank you for walking with me," he said, planting a kiss on top of my head that made me smile.

"You're welcome. Thanks for inviting me."

chapter eight

I STILL MIGHT KILL THIS BITCH.

Just for simply daring to exist in the same space as me.

This time, Nya wasn't doing anything particularly wrong – she hadn't said anything to me at all, in fact, offering nothing more than a slight sneer of acknowledgement. But the fact that, on a day I'd decided to venture to the coffeehouse for my regular people watching, she'd decided to make herself one of the people… it grated at me.

I'd chosen big, dark shades from my stash today, since we were having bright, sunny weather. Not that my eyes needed the sun protection, no. The shades were for camouflage – the weather made them not stand out as much.

Which was good.

Because the daggers I was staring into *Nya* and her equally shitty friend were vicious enough to earn me a restraining order, probably. Did I actually know anything about the woman she was sitting on a couch, cackling with? Of course not. But a wise person had taught me early on, bitches like that ran in packs.

I kept my expression stony, my gaze locked as they both, one by one, looked in my direction. Nya said something, and they both laughed as they openly stared.

Classic bullying tactic that I had to compel myself not to react to.

If *I* reacted, it would be with a level of force that landed me in jail.

"I don't think I've ever seen anybody grip a mug *that* tight."

A feminine voice drew my attention upward, to where a familiar face was standing near my chair.

"Jules, in case you don't remember," she said, her pretty face spreading into a smile as she took it upon herself to sink into the overstuffed chair beside me. "Tristan introduced you to a bunch of us at once, so I wouldn't be surprised."

I *had* been gripping my latte extra tight, channeling my anger through my fist, I guess. Putting it down on the table beside me, I returned Jules' smile and shook my head. "No, I wouldn't have been able to place your name, but I remember *you*. That beautiful haircut," I said, gesturing to where the flowers I recalled had already been replaced with a sunburst design.

"Perks of being booed up with the best barber in town," she laughed. "I see you know a little about that," she continued, pointing to where my tattoo was exposed due to my slouchy one-shoulder top. "Your ink is *gorgeous*. That's Tristan's work, right?"

"It is." My fingers went reflexively to the place where my rose was covered, even though it no longer evoked anything more than passing emotion. No matter how hard I stared, how long I looked, I couldn't see it in the mirror anymore. Apparently, the last of the memory was embedded in my fingertips.

"Eddie's protégé," Jules said. "I could be biased, but they're really the best in the business."

Whatever response I may have had to that was lost to

annoyance over another loud burst of laughter from Nya and her friend. I took in a deep breath, letting it out in a sharp exhale through my nose as I pressed my lips together to avoid yelling something ugly in their direction.

"*Ah*," Jules smirked. "I see we have a little something else in common too."

I raised an eyebrow at her, waiting for her answer.

"Nya and Mia over there," she said, openly gesturing, not caring if they saw her. "Or, like I prefer to refer to them – dumb and dumber."

I pulled my sunnies up, propping them on my head. "You don't like them either?"

"More like, they don't like me, so I'm giving them the same damn energy.

"Why don't they like you?"

Jules rolled her eyes. "Well, Mia used to fuck with Troy, casually, until he decided to stop... fucking with people casually. He wanted something serious... with *me*. But she felt like it should've been her, so she tried to mess with me, on some mean girl shit that I wasn't having."

"Yeah. Sounds familiar."

"Nya and Tristan used to kick it, so... I can imagine. It was before I moved back, so I don't really know much about it. I *do* know she beefed with Von."

"Von?"

"Tristan's *other* ex. High-school sweetheart, Kiara's mom..."

"Oh, right."

He'd mentioned her to me before.

"Maybe I should say *used* to beef with Von. Von beat her ass a couple years ago, and I don't think she's had a problem out of Nya since then."

"Damn, really?" I asked, eyes wide.

"*Mmmhmm*," Jules confirmed, with a wicked smile. "I don't

know the whole story, but Tris and Nya were dating at the time. I guess Nya got particularly flagrant or something, I don't know. But what I *do* know is that Von went to the salon and *dog walked* her in front of everybody. And then..." she broke off from her story to snicker. "Legend has it, Von climbed off her, straightened her clothes, looked at Nya and said... *I think your client's dryer went off.*"

"*Shut up!*" I yelped, letting out a loud burst of laughter I couldn't keep back. "Did she really?!"

Giggling, Jules shrugged. "If it's a lie, Nik is the one who told it. This was like a year before I came back, so I missed it."

"Came back?"

"Yeah," she nodded. "I was born here, then moved and lived in Cali for a while. Moved back, opened my business... found the love of my life," she grinned. "So... I'm pretty settled now. What about you? Has the rumor mill correctly spread that you bought that little candle shop across the street?"

Ugh.

I'd forgotten, kinda, about *that* element of staying in one place for an extended period. People remembered your face, then your name, then caught on to your routines, and started retaining details of your life.

Dangerous, for the life I used to live.

Now... it was part of blending into the neighborhood.

Deep cover, like Alicia said.

"Uh... yeah," I answered, smiling. "I got it all cleaned out, got some new supplies in there, all that."

"*Niiice.* You should let me come and shoot it for you."

My eyebrows went up. "Huh?"

"My bad – I'm a photographer," she explained. "*Love Notes.* I do all kinds of stuff – engagements, graduations, product shots, whatever, but what I really love is more like... lifestyle. Shooting people in their element. I'm already imagining you and this pretty ass face in like, a wax stained tee shirt, making candles, or just... I don't know, vibing in a caftan, testing new fragrances out."

"Wow," I laughed. "Your imagination is really vivid."

"It's not imagination – it's vision. I can *see* it. So... you in, or...?"

"I... don't know," I told her, shaking my head. "I'm not really into being photographed."

"I totally get that, not everybody is. So I won't pressure you," Jules assured. "But if you change your mind, or want some shots for a website or something, I've got you."

"Understood. Thank you."

"You're welcome. And hey," she said, leaning in. "Don't let those bitches get under your skin. Think about it, they're over there pretty as hell – both baddies, honestly. And yet, instead of using those good looks while they're in their prime, they're wasting it being petty and acting ugly, and they're still not gonna get the niggas they want. It's honestly pretty sad. Kinda makes you feel bad for them."

I snorted. "No the fuck it doesn't."

"You right."

At that, we both busted out laughing, and...

Damn.

I was turning into some kinda sap, because this benign ass interaction had shifted my mood pretty drastically.

I no longer felt like I might break my commitment to not murder someone.

"I've gotta get down to my studio for a session, so I'll see you later," Jules said, breaking into my thoughts with a claim that made me raise my eyebrows.

"Later? What's happening later?"

She gave me a confused look. "Nothing that I know of. I meant like... in general. Like I'll see you around."

"Oh. Shit. Sorry," I laughed, covering my face with my hands. "I... must need another latte or something," I said, trying to cover my awkward ass brain lapse.

"You're good," Jules chuckled, giving me a little wave as she headed off. When she was gone, I sat back into the plush softness of my chair, no longer concerned at all with the silliness of Nya and her friend.

I was thinking about *my* friends – or lack thereof – now.

Before I lost my nerve, and while I was still high on the chumminess of that interaction with Jules, I pulled out my phone.

"Hey. How are you?"

I sent that text to two different numbers in my phone – Penelope, and Dacia, both of whom I'd been a little too cavalier about keeping in contact with.

Well... *not* keeping in contact with.

Was it important for me to make friends with no connection to my past?

Yes, for sure... probably.

But, when I really thought about, it felt of equal importance to not be *so* committed to completely snubbing my past. As vital as it was for me to move forward and build this new life of my own, the fact remained that I would *need* people who really, *fully* understood what I was contending with.

And maybe more importantly... they might need me too.

"YOU READY TO MAKE THESE CANDLES?"

Those were the first words out of Tristan's mouth when he showed up, mostly unannounced, at the door of the candle shop.

"Make candles?"

"Yeah," he nodded. "You know... shit, I don't know anything about making candles to do my usual thing – you gotta do it for me."

I propped my hands on my hips as he stepped inside, closing the door behind him. *"You know, setting the wicks, melting the wax, mixing in the fragrance, pouring, test burning."*

"See?" he grinned. "Now I know you know all the steps. Let's make it happen."

"Um, hold up!" I called after him as he headed through the darkened shop to get to the workroom. The sunny weather from the last few days was gone, heavy rain and cloudy skies replacing the idyllic warmth and light, creating a gloominess that had definitely affected my mood since it arrived.

Tristan's busyness hadn't helped.

Not that I was mad or anything about it, I'd just... missed his face. Between an aggressive schedule at the tattoo parlor, increased security shifts, and making sure he spent ample time with his daughter, there hadn't been a chance for us to see each other in person.

And when he did show up, he wanted to talk about making goddamn *candles*?

He pretended he didn't hear me, getting all the way into the workshop before he stopped, putting a bag I hadn't really noticed down on the table.

"What's that?" I asked, distracted now that I'd followed him and gotten closer, and could smell something – other than him – that had me doing deep inhales.

"Late lunch. *But...* it's for after."

"After what?"

He gave me a dry look, crossing his thick arms in a way that made his tee shirt stretch quite nicely across his chest. "*After* we make these damn candles. So come on. What did you say the first step was?"

"I don't know," I shrugged, earning myself an even *more* scolding look.

"You telling me your ass hasn't watched *every* video on YouTube about making these damn candles?"

"Not *every*..."

"T... cut the shit."

"You can call me Temp now."

He smirked, shaking his head as he approached me, his larger frame dwarfing me in a way that would've made me wary back when I was still in service to the *Garden*. No matter how well-trained I was, that disparity in height and weight was a disadvantage to me, something I had to be mindful of in case I needed to defend myself.

That awareness would likely never go away completely, but now?

It was far, *far* at the back of my mind.

At least with *him*.

His arm snaked around my waist, drawing me close against his body as he tipped his head down. "Temp...," he murmured against my lips, "...you're not gonna distract *or* charm your way outta doing this."

"*Ugh*," I grunted, pushing away from him as he laughed. "Why are you doing this? I was perfectly fine to spend my rainy day binge-watching *other people* do this."

"You've spent enough time watching other people do what you want to be doing, I promise," he teased. "You're not gonna progress any further by doing that."

"Did anybody ask you?"

"Nah, but I'm telling you anyway," he countered, throwing his hands up. "So... come on, *Temp*. Where the wicks at?"

I couldn't help laughing, even though I was... feeling something I couldn't quite identify.

Nervous but excited but irritated but happy but overwhelmed but... willing.

Contentedly.

"Over there, in those boxes."

"And the jars?"

"In *those* boxes," I answered, pointing to a different spot. "And there are tools... um... spacers, I guess, that fit over the jars. To make sure the wick is centered."

Tristan nodded. "Okay. What else?"

"The wax flakes are in those cartons. It has to be melted to a specific temperature, and the fragrance oil has to be heated too. Not a lot, or you'll evaporate the fragrance. But if you do it right, it helps everything bind together, so you don't have any separating, or caving, or discoloration of the wax," I said.

"What else?"

"Then you let it cure. For at *least* three days, to let the fragrance oil really settle in. After that, you can do a test burn." I stopped talking when I realized how hard Tristan was staring at me, enthralled. "Why are you looking at me like that?" I asked.

"Like what?"

"Like... *that,*" I countered, gesturing at his face like I'd actually given more information. "Like you're... mesmerized or something."

"Shit, because I *am*. You *really* know this stuff, and that's... sexy."

"Knowing about candles is sexy?"

"No, the fact that you committed to something and learned all this stuff about it is. Now... let's see it through," he said, smoothing a hand through his beard. "I mean... unless you're gonna be pussy about it."

My head snapped back. "*Me?* Pussy? No sir. *Never* been that."

"I'on know... you seem a lil' bit pussy about these candles, but that's just *me,*" he challenged with a shrug and a smirk.

I started to threaten him with withholding *my* pussy, but that wouldn't work when he wasn't pressed about that anyway. I also considered kicking him out, but he'd probably take the food with him, besides the fact that I would probably seem even more like what he was accusing me of anyway.

I only had one real option – holding on to that *willing* feeling from a few minutes ago, instead of letting myself continue on the emotional rollercoaster.

"Grab a box of jars, some wick holders, some spacers, and some wicks. And get to loading," I told him, moving to the gas range to turn it on. "I'll melt a batch of wax for us."

A huge grin spread over Tristan's face and he opened his arms, gesturing for me to come to him.

I rolled my eyes about it, but obviously I went, and lost my battle against returning his smile as he squeezed me into a hug.

"Let's fuckin' *go*," he chuckled as he released me, then moved to follow the directions I'd given. I had this weird, unshakeable feeling in my chest as I grabbed the notebook I'd been using to jot down steps, tips, best practices, whatever... and then put it down, because I'd reviewed it so much I already knew exactly what to do, and had to stop stalling.

It was time to just make the fucking candles.

Even if I messed it up.

I... didn't though.

At least, I was pretty confident in thinking so by the time we followed all the steps I'd created from watching and reading countless tutorials and articles. We kicked our shoes off and worked, stopped to eat, then worked some more, then got everything cleaned up. And then... I stepped back from the ten candles we'd made, lined up on the worktable counter, and... blinked back happy tears.

Definitely turning into a sap.

"I believe you now," Tristan said, approaching me from behind to wrap his arms around me.

"Huh?"

He leaned in, propping his chin on my shoulder. "You said you weren't pussy. I can believe it now."

"I should kick you out, now that I've proven my non-pussiness," I told him, turning my head in his direction.

"You're too interested to kick me out," he shot back, moving in to nuzzle against my neck, and make me laugh. After a moment, he stopped being silly to press a kiss to my shoulder. "Seriously ... I'm proud of you."

"Me too."

I... really had actually *done* something.

Of course, it would take a few days – or more – to know if I'd *really* done it right or not, but in the meantime, I was calling this a victory.

A *needed* one.

I closed my eyes as Tristan kissed my shoulder again, taking full advantage of the skin displayed by the thin straps of the casual dress I'd thrown on. Soon, his mouth started a slow ascent, kissing from my shoulder to the curve of my neck, up my nape, and back around to my ear as he kept his arm anchored around me.

"What do you think we should do to celebrate your milestone?" Tristan asked, as his free hand crept up my thigh, under the hem of my dress.

"I... I don't... I don't know," I whispered, much too focused on his fingers tracing my clit through my panties to give a real answer.

"I think you *do*," he murmured in my ear, gently pushing my panties aside and finally, *finally* giving me the skin to skin contact I needed. Just a skim at first, and then a firmer swipe over my pussy, and then he sank his middle and pointer finger into me, pressing his thumb against my clit in a way that made my knees give a little. "Don't you?"

Shit.

I opened my mouth to respond, but couldn't seem to form actual words.

Not when it was imperative, as far as I was concerned, to not miss a single moment of the deep strokes of his fingers, his teeth and tongue and lips against my neck, his other hand moving up to caress my breast.

I'd never been happier to not be wearing a bra.

Especially once he tugged the top of the dress down to gain full access to my bare skin, to pinch and tug and tease my nipples in a way that made me even *more* sensitive between my legs.

It took me no time at all to combust.

"I really, *really* like watching you cum," he told me, not giving me a chance to even catch my breath before he'd turned me around to back me against the workroom table.

Once the cold steel was pressed against the backs of my thighs, he hefted me onto it, his head immediately dipping to catch a nipple between his teeth. My hands went to his locs, pushing his hair back so I could watch, enthralled, as my areola disappeared in mouth. He spread my legs wide, pushing his fingers into me again and taking advantage of the different angle to go deeper. I squirmed against his hand, whimpering my pleasure as he brought his mouth back to mine to swallow my scream as another orgasm hit me, *hard*.

"I think," Tristan said, when he finally pulled away from the kiss. "We should probably take these off you."

I only wondered for a moment what he was talking about before he was grabbing the waistband of my panties, pulling them off. I lifted myself so he could slide them over my ass before snatching them down my legs, and... putting them in his pocket.

I wrinkled my nose at him. "That's disgusting."

"You think so?" he asked, smirking as he lifted the fingers he'd had in my pussy and stuck them in his mouth, closing his eyes and grunting a little as he sucked the taste of me off them. He spread my legs again, stepping between them before he put his hand to the back of my neck, holding me there as he met my gaze. "I want to make you cum again. And again."

"Yes. *Please*." Was my immediate response.

He palmed my breast, giving it a slow caress before closing his thumb and pointer finger over my nipple, squeezing hard enough to make my pussy throb again. "Tell me what you want."

"You *know* what I want," I whimpered as he tugged again.

Tristan smirked, dropping his mouth to mine as he fished his wallet from the pocket *without* my panties in it. It got tossed somewhere once he'd maneuvered a condom out.

"I *guess* you've earned this today," he said, and I started to roll my eyes until he pulled his shirt over his head, finally confirming what I *thought* was underneath his clothes. He wasn't chiseled and carved, but he was *definitely* rock solid, and covered in beautiful ink that would have to wait for another time to explore.

My *whole* attention was needed for when he pulled down his shorts and boxers to reveal a thick, beautifully veined dick that most certainly did look like the kind you had to *earn.*

He chuckled at whatever he must've seen on my face as he grabbed the condom to put on.

"What?" I asked, shivering a little as he touched me to step between my legs, and rid me of the wrinkled dress I still, for some reason, had on.

"Your eyes went wide as fuck," he said, biting down on his lip as he teased me, rubbing the smooth, condom-sheathed head over my clit. "You've seen one of these before, right?"

"One of *these*? No," I answered, taking a fortifying breath as he lined himself up with my pussy.

He smirked, then pushed into me, filling me all at once with one firm stroke that snatched the air from my lungs. "Congratulations then... you deserve this."

I hooked my thighs around his waist, rolling my hips to match his rhythm. With my arms around his neck, I let my head fall back, feeling like I must've done something very, *very* right if Tristan's slow, deep strokes were what I deserved. He confirmed my assumption by grabbing the back of my neck again, dragging my mouth to his to whisper *"good fuckin' girl"* against my lips as he pumped harder.

Those words seemed to unlock a whole new level of wetness, a whole new depth. Tristan pushed deeper, matching his strokes to the lapping of his tongue against mine as he drove faster.

Deeper still.

Harder.

I was hanging on to whatever I could, his biceps, his shoulders, his waist, his locs, too overwhelmed to settle on any one thing, or actually... *anything*.

Which was fine.

He had it – had *me* – completely under control, every adjustment, every touch, every shift making me wetter, making me shiver, dragging what felt like every one of my nerves to the surface to be stimulated and treated to the same pleasurable rush.

Rush.

A perfect word to describe the feeling that swept over me gradually, and then all at once, making me lose the ability – and will – to breathe.

To see.

To think.

There was nothing but feeling, nothing but *heaven*, nothing but the flood of wetness and moans of pleasure and that slight, *blissful* moment of pain as he slammed into me one last time and stayed there, his hips pumping as *he* came.

"*Wow*," I whispered, when I could finally get my mouth and my brain back in sync.

Tristan chuckled as he pulled out of me, creating an absence I felt immediately. "I... feel *exactly* the same fucking way," he said, picking up his shorts, but handing me my dress back before he put them on.

Which... for some reason... kinda made my little bubble of post-orgasm bliss fade.

I pulled the dress on, and got myself down from the counter while Tristan put his clothes back on. Finally, watching him grab his shoes, I couldn't take it anymore.

"You didn't... suddenly stop liking me now that we've done that, right?" I asked, trying to keep my tone light like I was joking.

I wasn't.

Tristan straightened up, tucking the shoes under his arm without actually putting them on. "Huh?"

"You seem in a hurry," I explained, plastering on a smile. "And I was remembering your reasoning from a few weeks ago about why we *shouldn't* do this..."

His confused expression softened. "Temp... I honestly assumed we were taking this show upstairs. I mean... unless I'm not invited?"

"No, you're definitely invited, if you want. I just... this is dumb. Never mind," I said, shaking my head as embarrassed heat rushed to my face. Reminding me that, for as much *sexual* experience as I had... intimacy was foreign to me.

And I was making a damn fool of myself because of it.

"I... feel like I fucked this up somewhere," Tristan said, stepping toward me, and reaching out to grab me under the chin. "I'm sorry."

"You have nothing to apologize for," I assured. "It's... really not you. It's me. I'm making this weird."

He shrugged. "It doesn't have to be."

"I... it already *is*," I said, blinking back sudden, frustrated tears. "And I don't know how to—"

Fix it.

That would've been the rest of that statement if Tristan hadn't kissed me, effectively shutting me up.

"Let's order some dinner," he said, when he pulled back, not giving me a chance to go back to obsessing. "We can get cleaned up, watch some TV, eat. I don't know about you, but lunch feels like a long ass time ago," he added, making me laugh.

And... *shit.*

Somehow, just like that... I wasn't feeling quite so awkward anymore.

"Um... what do you want to eat?" I asked, a question he responded to with a suggestive lift of his eyebrows. "For *dinner*," I clarified, laughing again as he followed me up the stairs.

"Whatever your fine ass wants," he answered, from too close behind me, and then suddenly his arm was around me, making it awkward as hell to get up the stairs.

But it was fine.

Hell... it was *more* than fine.

Which was a new experience in itself.

chapter nine

THIS MAN IS A WORK OF ART.

I mean... I already knew he was *fine*, but the more I explored his body, intent on exhausting him to the point he couldn't even *think* about cumming again without losing his breath, it was just... *clear.*

Congratulations to me indeed.

My fingers skimmed the smooth, graffitied expanse of his skin – wide shoulders and thick biceps, solid midsection and strong thighs, all covered to varying degrees with beautifully inked illustrations.

The star of the show though was his dick.

On my knees in front of him, I took a moment to admire the weight of it in my hands before I tried my damndest to swallow it all.

It was a good, *good* feeling, his thighs tensed, his hands in my hair, cursing and barely containing himself from burying his dick in my throat.

And then, not containing himself at all.

His fingers grazed against my scalp, blazing little trails of further stimulation as he held my head in place, pumping into my mouth. I put one hand between my legs, the other between his, teasing my clit and his balls in the same uncontrolled pace – no rhythm, no thinking, just pure... pleasure.

Tristan tilted my chin up, adjusting me so he could plunge deeper into my throat, making me gag around him. Just teasing wasn't enough, so I pushed two fingers into my pussy, taking on his same frantic pace as he drove himself between my lips.

For every stroke, I sucked him hard – he cursed or groaned every time. I channeled my breathing through my nose, so a pesky lack of air couldn't get in the way of me trying my damndest to take him completely.

I was *so close* when he snatched me up from the floor.

"*Bring your ass here,*" he growled, his hand around my neck as he dragged my mouth to his, pressing his tongue between my lips to lap into me. He didn't let up as he backed me toward the bed, not until the mattress hit the back of my legs. Then, he tossed me down, climbing over me to sink between my thighs in a deep stroke that pulled contented moan from *both* of us.

This was how it was supposed to be.

Not going through the motions, not waiting for it to be over, not being on guard in case you suddenly had to defend your life.

Just... pleasure. And connection. And *relief.*

And probably protection, but we'd ran out of that and promptly decided not to let it stop the show.

I wanted all of him, everything, with nothing between us.

Luckily, he was willing to give it.

"*Shit,*" he cursed, panting, his large body spread across my bed as he tried to catch his breath. "You trying to kill me or something?"

I chuckled, sitting up beside him and *greatly* enjoying the appreciation in his gaze as it dragged over my nude body. "Just making up for the time between when I wanted your dick and when you actually gave it to me."

"I was *trying* to do the right thing."

"So this wasn't right?"

He scoffed. "It damn sure wasn't *wrong*."

"That's what I thought," I teased, leaning in for what I intended to be a quick press of our lips. Instead, he pulled me down against him, holding me close for a slow, perfect kiss that made me feel a little... dizzy.

Or something.

"Why are you doing me like this, knowing I need to get to the shop?" he asked against my lips, with his arm still tight around my waist.

"I didn't realize I was doing anything."

"You're a little too fine," he teased. "Making it *very* hard to stay out of you."

He said that, but still found the discipline to extricate himself from the bed – likely only because he was expected at the tattoo shop. He needed to go home first, for fresh clothes and all that too, so I didn't give a hard time about needing to go.

Besides... I probably already seemed pressed enough.

"Put something on so you can come lock the door," he insisted, so I did, following him down the stairs to the candle shop. "Hey – I meant to ask you yesterday – why the wood wicks for the candles?" he asked, gesturing around us at the empty shelves, even though the ones we'd made were still in the workroom.

I shrugged. "It was really something I wanted to try. When you burn the candle, it makes a sound."

"A *sound*?" he said, raising an eyebrow. "Why was my first thought of a candle screaming when you light it."

"Definitely not *that*," I laughed. "It's like..."

"Spoken word or something? Candles spitting bars?"

"*Shut up*," I giggled. "It's like a crackling sound, like a fireplace, fool. *Why* would you even think about candles reciting poetry?"

"I was trying to figure it out," he shrugged. "I'm thinking through the marketing plan. You said a sound, so shit, put those things up on open mic night, let's sell some candles."

"I *really* don't like you," I mused, grinning, as the thought of one of those damn candles, on a stool, behind a mic on stage played in my head. "Because now you've got me thinking of like... full on patchouli scent, making a candle that... smells like poetry. Which doesn't even make sense."

"It makes as much sense as you say it makes," Tristan countered. "Smell and taste are interconnected, so..."

"Don't encourage this. Cause now, I'm like... what if I make *all* the scents... poetic? The brand could be *Wax Poetic.* Or is that too corny?"

A little grin spread over his face. "Maybe *I'm* corny, cause... I actually kinda like it. But it also doesn't matter. Do *you* like it?"

"I... do," I admitted, wrinkling my nose as a wave of excitement rushed over me. It must've been really obvious on my face, because Tristan laughed, wrapping his arms around me in a hug.

"Congratulations baby," he said, planting a kiss on my forehead.

"*Baby*?" I lifted an eyebrow, looking him the face. "You get some pussy and I'm not T, or Temp, I'm *baby* now?"

He bit his lip. "I mean... unless you'd rather me *not*—"

"No, it's fine," I assured him. "I... like *that* too."

We said our goodbyes, and I let him go on his way while I tried my best not to fucking combust with happiness. Once the door was locked, I grabbed the mail that had been pushed through the slot, thumbing through it to make sure nothing of consequence was in there.

It was all junk, except for a copy of *Sugar & Spice* magazine.

The cover caught my attention because I recognized the couple – Kingston and Asha Whitfield, in a poker themed shoot. It was clear that Asha – the poker star – was the focus, since she was at the forefront, but Kingston sitting in the background, with their beautiful son in his lap, was not to be overlooked.

They were a beautiful family.

Alicia's family.

I knew her story well, of having been liberated from the *Garden* and brought to *Vegas* to work in a security role for the Whitfield family. It had taken time – and therapy, she said – but eventually she'd come to a place where she could settle into normalcy, whatever that meant for her.

It *really* gave me hope that the same thing was in my reach too.

As if I'd thought her up, Alicia's name and face came onto my screen as I headed back up the stairs to my apartment. I answered the call as I stepped through my door, headed straight for my favorite spot by the window.

"So he finally put you through the headboard like you wanted, huh?" Alicia asked, as soon as the call was connected and she could see me.

My mouth dropped open. "What?!"

She laughed. "You answered this phone smiling, hair all over your head, all kinds of hickeys on your neck and collarbone..."

"Yeah, he must've given her the business," Dacia said, only the top half of her head coming into view as she peeked at the screen.

They both looked at me, expectantly, waiting for an answer I had no intention of giving... only I couldn't actually help the big ass grin that spread over my face before I nodded, and they burst out laughing.

"I can't even *try* to lie to y'all. He was amazing. *It* was amazing. Everything is amazing," I gushed, and Alicia beamed at me from the screen.

"I'm *so* happy for you – and not because you got some dick," she laughed. "You really seem to be settling into this little space you've been carving, and that's a good thing."

I sighed, then shook my head. "I dunno. It feels.... Too good to be true," I confessed. "And I *know*, I'm not supposed to think like that, but I just... I'm trying to lean into the good, and enjoy it, but I'm worried something else is around the corner."

"Which is *normal*," Alicia reassured. "Hell, I have the same feeling *every day*. I would be more worried about you if you *didn't* feel like that."

"Yeah," Dacia added. "Even between me and Alicia, I struggle with it too. Don't beat yourself up over it – we were... *traumatized*. For *years*. That conditioning doesn't magically go away because we want it to."

I nodded. "Yeah, I get that part, completely, but... how do I get past it?"

"When you find out, spread the word," Dacia quipped, and we laughed.

"It's definitely a day to day thing," Alicia said. "Just take it day by day, and in the meantime... enjoy your honeymoon phase."

Using *honeymoon* was a stretch to refer to Tristan and me, but I understood her overall point, and had every intention of adhering to it.

Or at least *trying*.

I finished talking with Alicia and Dacia, forcing the conversation away from me and onto them. I didn't want this thing to be one-sided.

After I got off the phone, I grabbed some breakfast and flipped open that magazine, looking through the articles for something that might hold my interest. I smirked when my gaze landed on, *"Foolproof Ways to Keep Your Boo"*.

My *personal* relationship experience may have been lacking, but I was well-versed, generally, on what "kept" a man – he had to be obsessed, and even that was fleeting.

They were mine for the rest of their lives, though.

I flipped to the article, curious about what it might say, and had to smile when I saw the first lines.

If you're reading this, let me be the first to tell you – you can't keep anybody who doesn't want to be kept. Relationships are a mutual exchange, that should be based in respect, genuine affection, and enjoyment for all involved.

If you're feeling like you need to do something outside your sexual comfort, morals, dignity or safety, for the sake of "keeping" someone... reconsider. Love – and damn sure not "like" – should never require that.

But, if you're in a relationship where you're respected, cared for, supported, and loved, and feel the need to show some appreciation... we've got you! Here are a few moves you can consider:

- *Cook their favorite meal*
- *Play out their favorite fantasy*
- *Surprise them*
- *Facilitate some self-care time*

The list went on for a total of ten items, with each bullet followed by a paragraph of exposition and detailed suggestions.

It actually... wasn't that bad.

In fact, it was *so* "not that bad" that I got up and got myself together, to venture to the fresh market I'd come to love in the neighborhood.

grown.

Tristan was free again later this evening, so... maybe it would be a nice surprise to cook for him. I'd bet good money he wouldn't expect it.

In *grown*, I got my little basket and started exploring the aisles, trying to decide what I would fix. I kept things simple for myself, but I was willing to put the culinary skills we'd been taught in the *Garden* to good use. I mean, I was no gourmet chef by any means, but... I could make something happen.

I still hadn't quite yet decided what that *something* was gonna be yet when I turned another corner, spotting a familiar face.

"*Kiara*," I said, surprised to see Tristan's barely teenaged daughter out in a store in the middle of what I thought would've been a school day. "Why aren't you at school?"

Her eyes had gone wide behind her hot-pink glasses at the sight of me, and when she opened her mouth to answer, nothing came out.

"Uh, who the fuck are you?" I heard, and shifted my attention to Kiara's left, as another woman approached, scowling as she left her basket to get between me and Kiara.

I realized very quickly that Kiara and Tristan didn't look as much alike as I thought.

Because Kiara looked *just* like her mother.

Von, I remembered him calling her.

Von was... excessively pretty, with big brown eyes and long thick natural lashes, high cheek bones, cute nose. Like Tristan – and Kiara – she had locs, but hers were a pretty copper that contrasted against her deep brown skin.

Perfect skin.

"You hear me talking to you, right?" she asked, snapping her fingers in a sharp pop. "What did you have to say to my child that you couldn't say in front of me?"

I blinked. "I... um..."

"This is Tempest, mama," Kiara spoke up. "Daddy's girlfriend."

Those big brown eyes went damn near black, flashing in anger as she snapped her head back in my direction. "*Excuse me*? I don't know *what* Tris told you that has you all comfortable addressing my child, but let me tell you something – you don't know *her* until you know *me*, and I don't fucking know you. And you can tell Tristan I thought he learned his lesson with the last bitch he had around my daughter – don't let yourself be another lesson he has to learn with me, 'kay?"

All that came pouring out of her at what felt like lightning speed, and I was still so dazed I could barely process what was happening.

I *did* hear the menace in her tone, though.

"Who the fuck do your call yourself threatening?" I asked, unable to keep a smirk off my face. "You're right – you *don't* know me, or you'd *know* better."

Her eyes went wide. "*Oh*, so he got a bitch with some backbone this time, okay, that's cute. But you're still trash for being around my kid without even the courtesy of having said *hi, bye, kiss my ass,* whatever, *beforehand*."

"She hasn't been *around me*, mama," Kiara spoke up again, before I could give the ugly response that was right on the tip of my tongue. "We ran into her one day in *Urban Grind,* and I could tell he liked her, so I made him tell me. That's all. And she asked why I wasn't at school," she explained, clearly trying to diffuse the tense situation. "I had an orthodontist appointment, so I got to skip school."

"Oh." That was Von's dry ass response. "My bad."

Without anything more, she turned and walked away – not an apology, nothing. Kiara gave me a sympathetic shrug, then ran off to follow her mother, leaving me to wonder what the fuck had just happened.

Well, obviously I *knew* what had just happened, but damn. What a mood killer.

I left *grown* without buying a single grocery, because by mind was reeling now.

Of course this thing between Tristan and I was very new, so it was sensible – smart, even – that he hadn't had me around his daughter.

But to not have even mentioned me to his child's mother over the weeks he'd spend working himself into my presence... kinda bothered me.

You're probably tripping.

Right.

That was probably it.

But... just in case, since I didn't end up with the things for cooking... I decided to pull something different from the list.

Instead of wallowing in confusion, I set my sights for the tattoo parlor, knowing – hoping – that seeing him in person would cheer me up.

A quick drop in to surprise him could be a perfect midday energy boost for both of us.

chapter ten

It was quiet when I walked into the tattoo parlor.

Most likely because it was midday and the people who were in there now for their ink were people who had set up appointments with their individual artist.

Which was why Tristan was here in the first place - an appointment he hadn't said too much about.

That gave me a little bit of pause about this whole "surprise" thing, *especially* since it said nothing about popping up at someone's job. I didn't want to be too big of an interruption or distraction while he was trying to work, but...still.

After that little run-in with the mother of his child, I was feeling a little out of sorts. Add to that the sensitivity of us having finally had sex, and I was just confused. And not nearly as secure as I would have liked to be.

So... I pushed past my little doubts and sauntered up to the front desk anyway.

The same person who was there when I initially went to get my tattoo was there at the front desk again.

Priya.

She smiled when she saw me, recognizing me as a former customer.

"Hey, you back for some more ink?" she asked.

"Oh no, not today," I told her, pressing my fingers into the cold surface of the desk. "I actually popped by to see if I can talk to Tristan for a minute. I mean, if he's available."

For some reason, that made Priya roll her eyes. "I mean, he's back there with a customer, but he ain't busy. You can go back there."

"Oookay." I thought, but gave her a smile and nodded before I took her at her word that Tristan wasn't actually busy.

Maybe he was taking a break, or maybe he was tattooing one of the other artists that worked there in the shop, so it was a casual thing.

Or... maybe he had his face in Nya's crotch as he tattooed her upper inner thigh.

This whole not killing people thing was getting harder and harder as this day wore on.

"Oh hey Temp," Nya chirped, looking up at where I was standing in the open doorway.

It made me feel a little better that the door was open for this, implying that there wasn't much privacy needed, but still... this wasn't exactly the kind of scene I wanted to walk up on.

"That's kind of funny, isn't it? Temp like *temporary*. Only for now, not really anything serious you know?" She kept talking, only irritating me further.

"So it's going to be *real* serious when I beat your ass then?" I asked, not even remotely capable of exercising any type of real restraint against simple words.

My rebuttal, not her slick comment was the thing that finally made Tristan look up from what he was doing to notice I was there, stopping the tattoo gun to give me that censoring look.

"Babe, chill," he said. "Nya is fucking around."

"Yeah, she's gonna fuck around and get my foot up her ass," I countered. "I'm not her damn friend, so, she can find somebody else to play with."

"Oh so serious and violent. I didn't know you were into that, Tristan," Nya went on, still needling.

"Well maybe the mother of his child beating your stupid ass should have clued you in."

Nya gasped, and Tristan groaned, putting the tattoo gun down completely and standing up from his seat between her legs.

"I'll be right back," he told her, not looking back as he hooked his hand around my arm to drag me from the open doorway to an empty break room. "Is this how it's going to be now?" he asked, clearly annoyed with *me* for some reason. "This is exactly why I wanted to hold off. We've had sex, we crossed that line, and now the drama starts."

"And that's my fault?" I asked. "I'm the one bringing the drama? A few hours ago you had your dick down my throat, and now I walk up in here and you're face deep in your ex's pussy while she throws little jabs, and somehow the drama is *my* fault?"

"Man *come on* with the exaggerations T," he groaned. "Yes, me and Nya used to date, but we don't anymore. She's a friend who wanted some ink. I was supposed to say no to that because of what me and you have going on?"

"*Don't* try to twist it to make it sound like I'm being ridiculous. A typical friend? No, it wouldn't be a problem. But when this *friend* very clearly wants to be more than that, and has no issue openly antagonizing the person you're seeing? Yeah it's a problem."

"Temp, how is it different from *any other* customer? I've got to run my client by you beforehand to make sure there's not somebody you don't like on it?"

"Okay so is she a friend, or a client? Did she pay for the tattoo?"

Tristan frowned, confused. "I don't know what that has to do with anything, but yeah, she's paying - we... barter, I guess. She keeps my locs together for me."

My eyes damn near ballooned out of my head at *that*. "Ohhhh, so she pays by getting to be up close and personal with you for hours and hours at a time. Got it."

"You are *completely* fucking bugging right now! If me and you are together, I can't have friends?"

"That's not what I'm saying."

"Then what *are* you saying?"

"I'm saying that... if me and you are together, you can't have *that* friend," I shrugged. "Because that bitch is not a friend - she's a parasitic ex hanging in hopes of becoming more again, and antagonizing any future prospects along the way."

I knew this from professional experience - I'd neutralized my fair share in order to get the access I needed to a target.

"*Wow*. We've known each other a few weeks, and now you're telling me who my friends are?"

I let out a dry chuckle. "Obviously you need *somebody* to. Do you have long conversations about life with her? She supports your dreams? Checks in with you? Makes sure you're okay? Could you count on her for help if you were in trouble? *Anything* of that nature?" I asked, digging into my point. "Cause if the answer is no to any of that, and you can't think of anything equivalent, that's not your fucking friend - it's a bitch you keep around to feed your ego, and you know... I won't deal with that."

He scoffed. "Deal with *what?*'"

"With not being a priority for you. That's how relationships work, right?"

"So you feel like you should be my top priority now?"

"I didn't say top, I said *a* priority. If this means anything to you, at all."

Tristan's face wrinkled into a scowl. "Of course it does, why would you even say that shit?"

"Because before I got here, I got cursed out by the mother of your child because I spoke to your daughter and she had no idea I existed. Then I get here, and you're up your ex's crotch, letting her speak to me any fucking kinda way," I explained, feeling ridiculous once I'd said it out loud, but... nah.

Fuck that.

My feelings didn't have to -weren't *about* to - be downplayed

"We're still figuring this out, so no, I haven't told Von anything about you. Why were you talking to them anyway?"

"I ran into them at the store. And it's not even really about that - I'm not mad about that. I'm mad because when I came here looking for some reassurance, I found you with your ex."

"Conducting business."

"It's not fucking business!" I countered. "It's not business, and she's not your friend. What she *should* be is a non-factor."

"And you don't feel like this - your whole reaction to all this - is extreme?"

"I feel like you're trying to make me feel crazy so that you can go about doing the exact same shit you've been doing," I told him. "I feel like you're being purposely obtuse. Or did you forget you snatched an *actually* innocent man out of my face at the coffeehouse? Meanwhile you wanna scold me for threatening Nya like she wasn't antagonizing me."

"It's not the same!"

"You're right, it's not - it's *worse*. You couldn't take the idea of me entertaining someone else, while I'm supposed to be cool with *your* shit!"

"Nothing is gonna happen between me and Nya!"

"Does *she* know that?" I asked. "Because it doesn't seem

like it to me. And the fact that you're so resistant to even the *idea* of not encouraging her bullshit? Is a massive red flag to me."

"So we're back around to you telling me who I can talk to?"

"No, I'm back around to telling you what *I* won't deal with," I snapped. "And it's exactly *this*. This thing between us is new, and fragile, and yet your connection to your ex is your clear priority. *Not* what might be happening with us. And I don't accept that. I may be new to my own relationships, but I'm *very* well-versed in bullshit. And for all your charm and whatever the fuck else... you're full of it."

Tristan blew a heavy breath through his nostrils. "So...what are you saying? If I don't fall in line with whatever demands, you don't wanna do this anymore?"

I shook my head, fully irritated, but also...resigned. "No. I'm saying that I won't settle for you maintaining a relationship with an ex who has such clear disdain for me. I'm setting the tone right now. If your supposed friendship with her is more valuable to you than what could be with me...I suggest that's what you should give your attention to."

With that, I turned to leave, easily shaking Tristan off me when he tried to stop my exit.

"T, hold up," he asked, but I shook my head as I stepped through the door.

"You let me know what you decide is more important to you."

When I turned the corner to leave, the first face I saw was Nya, grinning from the doorway of Tristan's inking room.

"Trouble in paradise?" She asked, clearly thrilled to have been the catalyst for friction between me and Tristan.

That smile dropped from her face as I headed straight for her.

I wasn't even thinking anymore - what was there to think

about? I was sick of this bitch and I needed her to feel it in a way that words didn't seem to get through to her.

Like my hand around her neck.

Like *both* hands around her neck, while she wasted what little breath she had screeching and flailing helplessly until Tristan and another artist managed to pry me off her.

Damn shame.

"Sh-she tried to kill me!" Nya sputtered, her face streaked with tears as she scooted across the floor where she'd fallen to get away from me.

"If I was trying to kill you, you'd be dead," I told her, shaking the hands off me and then stomping back down the hall toward the exit.

"Temp, what the fuck was that?!" Tristan called after me, following me down the hall.

"It was me making a point - I bet she won't say shit else to me," I shrugged.

"Yeah but she might press charges."

"And I'll beat her ass for real then. *Fuck her.* Or hell, maybe I shouldn't say that to you."

He sucked his teeth. "Man, come on with that shit."

"No *you* come on. Unless I'm still being unreasonable."

From there, I really did leave, exhausted at this point of having this circular conversation with him. He wasn't interested in seeing past his own bullshit, and I wasn't interested in accepting it.

And I *hated* how this whole thing was making me feel.

I'd gone from floating on a cloud of orgasmic bliss to... whatever the fuck *this* was.

But still, I refused to go along with whatever got dished in my direction. I liked Tristan - a lot.

A whole lot.

However, my inexperience didn't mean I was stupid.

I'd seen and acted out entirely too much to fall for the usual shit.

That didn't make it not hurt though.

It took until I was back at the candle shop - without groceries or a lover - that it really hit me. Such a drastic range of emotions over the course of barely half a day... Could that be good for *anyone?*

Back in my apartment, I pulled out my phone to call Alicia, again.

"I should kill him I think," I said, as soon as she answered the phone.

"That was a fast honeymoon period," she said. "What happened?"

"He...shit, I don't know how to explain it," I admitted. "But I hate how I feel right now. I hate it. So I should kill him."

"Killing him wouldn't solve anything," Alicia countered.

"It would solve literally *everything.*"

"Tempest... stop, okay? Just tell me what's wrong?"

I blew out a big sigh, dropping to the edge of the bed with my eyes closed. "His ex. Well...his *exes*. He has a kid, and obviously she has a mother. She's not really the problem though."

"Okay... So what is then?"

"The more recent ex. And the fact that he's still involved enough with her that she feels comfortable making slick comments that he won't check. And not just that - he was tattooing her, and she does his locs for him, and openly flirts, and he doesn't see a problem with any of it. He expects me to be okay with it. And since I'm *not* okay with it, he's acting like I'm... like I'm overreacting for not accepting this bullshit."

Alicia pushed out a sigh. "Yeah, sounds about right, based on... damn near everything I know, have read, have heard, have *seen* from men. It's common. So... welcome to normalcy."

"Cree wouldn't do this type of shit."

"Cree is a grown ass man. He's got a decade on your little friend over there," Alicia laughed. "He was probably doing the same shit at twenty and thirty - and let's not overlook the fact that he literally has a child with my friend."

"But you all handle it like adults, which makes it work."

"True. But I thought you said his daughter's mother *isn't* the problem?"

I sighed. "She's not. It's this other bitch. Who...I may or may not have choked?"

"Tempest!"

"I'm sick of her mouth!" I defended, even though I knew it was weak. "And I... don't like that Tristan seems so attached to her. Or that he didn't seem to have a problem with her talking shit to me, but the moment I opened *my* mouth, it was a problem."

"That would piss me off too."

"Right?! So I just... I don't know. I feel like this is already over, before it even really started. Just this morning, I was so enthralled, so..."

"Dick whipped?"

I laughed. "Yeah, if you wanna call it that. But now... It's like I've seen too much to be willing to accept this Nya woman as part of some package deal when it's not like she's this great friend to him or something."

"And you don't have to!" A new voice chimed, making me sit straight up. "Temp, it's Loren. Alicia stepped out to take this call but I'm nosy and her phone is up loud."

I chuckled.

Loren was *the friend* Cree had a child with -a bubbly, straightforward doctor who Cree knew before he and Alicia were a thing.

Yeah, I was all in their business.

So it didn't bother me for Loren to be in mine, especially if she was about to give me something useful.

"Listen honey - you're new to this relationship stuff, right? I know it feels like a drawback, but it's not -cause you're not jaded and worn down yet. So many of us have been subjected to men's manipulations and gaslighting to the point that it feels normal. As if we should *expect* our feelings not to matter, so we swallow them to seem cool or unbothered, but fuck that. *Having a man* is not the only good thing in life. It's barely top fucking five. Or hell, ten. He wants to grin in another bitch's face, cool. Find one who won't. Or don't. Whichever way, you'll be fine."

"Yeah," Alicia said, after a moment had passed to absorb Loren's words. "What she said."

I pushed out another sigh. "I get it. I just... Was really into him. But I guess it would've been silly to think my first... *thing* might be the only one."

"It's not silly at all," Alicia said, her tone soothing. "It's sweet. And it's only been a little time since all this happened - don't jump all the way out the window. Tristan could surprise you."

"Thinking that is how I got into this trouble in the first place," I argued. "Thinking he could surprise me, instead of relying on how predictably disappointing most men are."

"Ain't that the truth," Loren agreed, making Alicia laugh. "Don't you have a whole fiancé?"

"Yeah, but I'm talking about these other niggas, not him."

The two of them went back and forth a bit, laughing, and trying to offer me more advice, but really...I was over it.

By the time I got them off the phone, I was fully past all the anger and had settled knee deep into sadness.

chapter eleven

"Ay braces, why you going so fast! Slow up! Where you going?"

"Let me walk you home lil mama! I can walk you all the way to your room. We can play doctor, whatever!"

"I said leave me alone!"

I'd had every intention of ignoring the loud ass street harassment happening in front of the shop next to mine - not the boutique, but on the other side. There was nothing there, and people often took to using it as a hangout spot no one would complain about.

I wasn't about to listen to what sounded like a young woman getting hassled though.

I stepped out of the candle shop door as the whole group turned a corner - with *Kiara* of all people leading the crowd.

Or rather, being stalked.

Her face was pulled into a scowl, earbuds pushed deep in her ears - both defense mechanisms. Anger to mask the fear the young men following her were causing, earbuds to drown them out as they surrounded her, impeding her from getting home.

At the sight of me, more than one let out a wolf-whistle, but I wasn't with that shit.

"Y'all heard her say to leave her alone, right?" I snapped, stepping between her and the four older boys - one of whom wasn't a boy at all, but a grown ass man - and a familiar one, at that.

The same motherfucker from my first night out in the Heights.

"This don't concern you, bitch," he spat in my direction, pulling a smile to my lips.

"Kiara... go inside," I told her, gesturing inside the shop.

She didn't hesitate, just slipped past me into the safety of the shop.

Smart girl.

"Do y'all know how old she is?" I asked, mostly addressing the one who was *way* too old to be bothering Kiara, even though they all were, really.

"That ass looks full-grown to me," he sneered.

"You *stay the fuck away from her,*" I lobbed right back at him, stepping fully into his face, not giving a shit about a size or height difference. "She's thirteen years old. I will kill you myself."

"You won't do sh--*AYY*, what the fuck!" He shrieked, backing up as I brandished a blade in his face. "Yo, what's your problem?"

"You, and niggas *like you* are my problem," I explained, looking at the others too. "Maybe if you're worried about getting your dick filleted, you'll learn how to leave people alone."

"You ain't gone do nothing with that," the ringleader claimed, boldly taking a step back in my direction. I didn't hesitate - I sliced through the front of his tee shirt, giving just enough pressure to touch his skin.

To prove a point.

The peanut gallery all started shouting, two of them taking off running at the sight of the tiny bit of blood I'd drawn.

Pussies.

"You really fucking cut me!"

I shrugged, frowning at the soiled blade. "I really fucking did. You may wanna find some fucking business before I take another slice."

To emphasize my point, I fake lunged at him, and just like the *bitch* I knew he was, he flinched, then he and the other fool took off running too.

Predictable.

I turned back to the store to find Kiara staring out the window, having watched the whole exchange.

"Wow. You're such a badass," she gushed as I entered the shop, locking the door behind me. "You really are an assassin, aren't you?"

"Do those guys always bother you like that?" I asked, avoiding the question.

"Not always. I take a different way home every day, so nobody can figure out my routine."

Smart girl.

"Do you know them?"

"Not really, besides seeing them around the neighborhood sometimes. They're always saying stuff to me," she admitted, in a clearly uncomfortable tone as she gripped the straps of the hot pink backpack that matched her braces.

Which *really* pissed me off.

There was no way to mistake this little girl for anything other than exactly that - a little girl.

Not that "looking older" than her age would make the behavior okay, but the headband, hot pink everything, and obvious youth in her face made it feel so much more insidious.

"Have you said anything to your parents? To...your father?" I asked, propping a hip against a display as I waited for her answer.

"Daddy would kill him. All of them," she answered, her tone so matter of fact that it almost felt like "*duh bitch are you stupid?*"

And maybe I was, for asking that question at all, when the answer was far from surprising.

"Well yeah...he'd try to make sure they didn't bother you anymore."

Kiara shook her head, taking it upon herself to remove her backpack and take a seat on an empty counter. "He wouldn't *try*. He'd make sure."

"Okay, so what's the problem?"

"He'd have to go away again, and I like it a lot better when he's here. When I can see him."

Oh.

Right.

I'd only known Tristan a short time, so had no experience coping with him being deployed - Kiara and her mother had been the ones managing the care packages and video calls and all that - assuming he'd even been allowed any of those.

They'd definitely had to manage the fear that he might not actually make it back home.

"So you just...take it? Because you're scared of what might happen if you tell somebody?"

She shrugged. "What else can I really do? They never touch me or anything, and I've always been able to get away from them so they can't follow me all the way home."

"So you think."

Her eyes went wide over my correct - but likely terrifying - input. "I didn't think they were smart enough for something like that."

"Probably not," I assured her. "But diligence is important

either way. You can't be too careful. And you should definitely say something to *someone*. Maybe your mom?"

"You met my mom. She's more likely to wind up in jail than daddy."

Yeah, that tracks.

"I get it, Kiara. But... You have to tell someone. In case - God forbid - something happens."

Her big brown eyes came to me, blinking hard. "I'm telling *you*."

I frowned. "No. I'm not... You're not... I... Your Dad and I aren't even together," I blurted. "So... I probably shouldn't be the person to hold this information for you."

Kiara raised an eyebrow at me. "*Really*? I mean I knew he was all sad and stuff, and my mom cussed him out, but I figured everybody would get over it. I thought grown-ups were supposed to be mature?"

"I'm mature!" I argued, hella defensive... with a tween. "It's just... You're not old enough to understand."

"Sure I am, my dad was being a fuckboy and it made you mad."

"Do your parents know you're cursing like this?!"

"No," she giggled. "But my mom was the one who said it - about daddy acting like a fuckboy," she explained, very comfortable with the term. "At first she was cussing him out for not telling her he was dating somebody, then he started trying to explain, and told her what happened at DistInk'd, which... He should've known better. My mom always goes nuts about Nya. She really doesn't like that lady."

I bit down on my lip, chewing a little as I tried to contain my curiosity. I really had no business having this conversation - *any* conversation - with Tristan's child.

Especially since I'd been ignoring the fuck out of him for over a week now.

But lil sis had all the tea, and I wanted it.

"Does… Your mother always get mad about him having girlfriends?"

Kiara shook her head. "Nope. Just Nya. And she was cool about Nya at first, but… you've met Nya, so…"

"Yeah."

"That's why she was so mean to you at the store that day," Kiara explained. "She's still shellshocked from Nya."

"How old are you again?" I asked, crossing my arms.

"Thirteen," Kiara giggled. "I read a lot."

What?

"Anyway, my mom was all, *I told you that bitch was nothing but trouble, but you don't wanna listen. And so on.*"

"Uh huh."

"And then she was like, *no woman who values herself worth a damn is gonna be cool with a slut puppy like Nya in your face unchecked, so if you want to be serious, you have to make a decision.*"

"Wait, back up," I said, raising my hands. "Slut puppy?"

Kiara shrugged. "My mom has all kinds of insults for Nya."

Maybe I do like her, after all.

"Whatever - I hope your daddy - and your mother, and *you* know, that even if he does decide to drop his little *friend*… she's not his biggest problem. *He* is." I stopped again, shaking my head. "*Why* am I talking to a child about this? Actually - did he send you?"

Kiara's face twisted in confusion. "Huh? You called me in here…"

Oh.

Right.

My point still remained.

Nya was a grown ass woman, in control of her own actions. Tristan wasn't in charge of her. And *really* I didn't even care about them remaining friends after their relationship was over.

My problem was with the way *Tristan* hadn't set any real boundaries with her.

He gave her the access and confidence to feel like she could challenge and disrespect me where he was concerned. Could he make her do or not do anything?

Of course not.

But he set the tone, creating an environment where her bullshit was tolerated and accepted instead of treating it like the open hostility it was.

I'd been through too much to finally start living on my own terms to settle for a man who made another woman's comfort paramount to mine.

His daughter?

Sure, I'd gladly take a backseat.

Even his mother, and the mother of his child within reason.

But Nya?

That shit was a nonstarter.

"I don't think he knows how to let people go."

Kiara's voice pulled me from my thoughts, and I raised an eyebrow at her, confused.

"Huh?"

"You know he was in the military, right?" She asked, and I nodded my assent. "After last time - the last deployment - he was different when he came back."

"Different how?"

"Kinda... sad, I guess?" she shrugged. "He doesn't really talk about it, and he's a lot better now, but mama told me a lot of his friends died. Like he *saw* them die. And I think that's why he's still friends with Nya. He doesn't wanna lose anybody. Even when they're annoying."

I stood there, open-mouthed from that revelation as Kiara hopped down from the counter and returned her backpack to her shoulders.

"Anyway, thanks for the rescue. Sorry you had to out yourself."

"Out myself?" I asked, following her to the door.

She looked back at me, wearing a self-satisfied grin.

"Yeah. As an assassin. Why else would you randomly have a blade to like...ninja slice somebody with?"

I laughed. "Well, there are these things called boxes, that sometimes need to be opened, and-"

"My dad told me what tattoo you got covered."

Those words were like getting doused with a bucket of cold water.

"*What did you just say*?" I hissed, slipping quickly between her and the door.

She shrank back. "I'm sorry!"

"Tell me what the fuck you're talking about, little girl."

"Th-there were these...stories. It was on this site for fiction, but the author implied that it's based on true stories. They're all about like... espionage and murder and...sex," she added, in a very, very quiet tone. "And one of the details is that, all the women have a rose tattoo."

What the fuck...

"*Show it to me*," I demanded, knowing she likely had a cell phone on her.

"I can't," she insisted. "It got pulled down, which made me think it must really be true! It was like a year ago, and I feel like it probably wasn't one of the actual assassins, just someone who knew about it and-"

"Your mouth is gonna get you in trouble," I interrupted her, as it suddenly occurred to me how incredibly guilty I was acting. "And your imagination too."

Her eyes went wide. "I won't shrink myself just because -"

"Nobody fucking said all that lil girl," I snapped, moving away from the door. "I didn't say you had to stop, I said it was gonna get you in trouble. So you should think about that. Instead of blurting made up stories to a woman you don't know, but think might be an assassin."

"*Former* assassin," she corrected. "And you wouldn't hurt a child."

"Wanna bet?"

"Yep," she grinned. "You didn't cover it to protect or conceal yourself - you did it to reinvent yourself. So you're not an assassin anymore, just my dad's girlfriend."

"I'm *not* your dad's girlfriend. Or an assassin either."

"Sure. Those things don't define you, you're Tempest. Your own woman. Those are just threads that make up your fabric."

"Get out of here," I demanded, pointing out the door. "And I'm definitely telling whichever of your parents I see first about those guys following you."

"I figured that," she shrugged, pushing the door open. "*Your* secret is safe with me though."

I woke up before the glass broke.

There was just... This feeling of unease that ripped me from my sleep, guiding my fingers to the slick black gun tucked between the headboard and the mattress.

I had it in my hands, had turned the safety off, had swung my feet out of bed, onto the cool surface of the hardwood.

And then there it was.

The unmistakable crash of someone breaking in.

I was light on my feet, quick to do a cursory sweep around the apartment to make sure I was alone before tossing on some pants to go with the oversized shirt I'd slept in, and shoes.

Then I opened the door.

Quietly, of course.

No lack-of-oil whine from any of my hinges, no alerting creek from the stairs. Once upon a time, I was heralded for my stealth, so it was almost fun getting down those stairs, using the second entrance to make sure there was no one in the workroom.

Almost.

There *was* still an intruder to contend with.

At first, I thought whoever it was had already moved on, but then I realized there was a dark figure lurking half-crouched near the door.

If they were from the *Garden*, they would know better.

This had to be someone else.

But at least it wasn't worst-case scenario.

The figure suddenly moved, grabbing one of the removable shelves from the wall. From my concealed position in the stock room, I watched as that shelf got used like a battering ram through the glass front door, making even more noise as it shattered and rained down.

Trying to draw my attention.

A skilled hunter wouldn't have needed to break a thing, and wouldn't have wanted the attention on them. This person probably thought they couldn't get past my apartment door on their own, so they had to draw me out instead.

Well...

Here I was.

"You looking for me?" I asked, my voice commanding as I took a wide stance in the workroom doorway, gun aimed. The only illumination spilled in from the streetlights through the broken door and window, but it was enough for that dark figure to see me - and my loaded weapon - and decide it was better to run.

"HEY!" I shouted, taking off after them, making it to the

sidewalk in front of the shop before I lifted my gun, aimed, and...didn't take the shot.

I couldn't fire a fucking gun in the middle of the neighborhood without attracting a lot more attention than I wanted.

With two gaping holes in my storefront, the block was already hot enough.

Still on high alert, I retreated back to the workroom - my best vantage point - to pull my phone from the pocket of the sweats I'd tossed on. My eyes stayed focus around me, seeking out movement as I tucked the phone between my ear and shoulder to keep my hands free.

"Hello?"

I frowned at the sound of the male voice on the other end of the line until he repeated himself, and recognition struck me.

"Cree? Why are you answering Alicia's phone? Did something happen to her?"

"Some of her homegirls and five too many margaritas happened to her," he chuckled. "She is knocked the fuck out, but when the phone woke me up and I saw it was you, I figured I should answer. Are you okay?"

"I...I don't know," I admitted. "Somebody broke into the shop. Then ran when I confronted them."

"Confronted?? Did you shoot anybody?"

"No!" I rolled my eyes. "I wanted to, but I knew better, and now I... don't know what to do. I didn't have a plan for something like this. I *should've* had a plan for something like this," I said, even though that last part was more for myself than him.

"Call the police."

"What would I do that for?"

"So that if whoever it was comes back, you'll have an explanation for shooting them."

"They can't come back for me if I'm not here."

"But you will be there, because this is your life now, remember? You can't just jet anymore," Cree said, his tone stern, but still gentle. "Stuff like this happens to anybody, all the time. You gonna pull your roots up and run away?"

"Fuck you."

"You're welcome," he chuckled in response. "Call the police, so they can file the little report, and I'm gonna talk to Willow about making sure all your documentation is in order for your gun. You're a regular citizen, Tempest, so that should be reflected in your response to this."

"Oh, so I should expect the police to beat my ass and accuse *me* of breaking in then?"

Cree busted out with a full laugh this time. "Nah, not in the *Heights*. I hear you though. I get it. I don't *think* you're gonna run into that there."

I pushed out a sigh, denying the urge to make an unfair quip about him being a cop - he'd quit the force in Vegas because he was disgusted with them, so it would be a low blow to take it there.

Especially when he was trying to help.

Especially when... He wasn't wrong.

"Fine. I'll call," I conceded.

"Good. As soon as Alicia is conscious, I'll update her on what's going on."

I thanked Cree and we said brief goodbyes, so I could get *MHPD* on the line. It was a small operation, so I was impressed by how fast they arrived.

I still couldn't wait for them to leave.

I was tired, and anxious, and annoyed, and... Just not at all in a good space. All I wanted was for them to stop asking questions, stop poking around, stop *being here* so I could crawl back into my bed and pretend the world didn't exist for a few hours.

Of course that was wishful thinking.

There was no way I'd be able to relax now.

"Tempest!"

I was still standing outside, waiting to be left alone when I heard my name. When I looked up, Tristan was headed toward me, his arrival decorated by the steady red and blue flashes from the police cars.

Ah hell.

"What happened?! Are you okay?" He asked, removing his jacket to wrap around my shoulders, making me realize for the first time how much the temperature had dropped for the night.

It was warm, and it smelled like him, so I decided not to shrug it off.

"What are you doing here? It's like four in the morning," I said, taking a step back to put some distance between us. It was coming up on two weeks since we'd spoken, and the longer I ignored him, the easier it was.

At least, it had been.

Now that he was in my face, it was a bit of a different story.

"I was at the shop, finishing a big piece for a client," he explained. "Neither of us wanted to spend a second day on it, so we toughed it out."

"Oh."

He raised an eyebrow. "You gonna tell me what's going on, or?"

"Nothing. Somebody threw a brick through the window, and broke up the door. I think they were trying to get me to come down, but I kinda snuck up on them, and they ran."

Tristan's eyes went wide. "Trying to get you to come down? For what? Who was it?"

"Obviously I don't know the answers to any of that."

"I know, it's just...." Tristan blew out a sigh. "Aiight, pack yourself a little bag. You're gonna come with me."

"I am?"

"Well, you damn sure can't stay *here*. It's not safe."

"But I'd be safe with you?"

He frowned. "What? *Yes*."

"Really?" I challenged. "Nya isn't crashing on the couch too, is she?"

"Will you just go pack the goddamn bag?"

"*No*, actually, I won't," I told him, snatching his jacket off my shoulders to shove at him. "You don't get to run up in my face playing superhero after that bullshit you pulled with me."

"You're gonna act like I haven't tried to talk to you?"

I scoffed. "Yeah, got your messages about wanting to *talk*, but honestly Tristan, *fuck talking*. There's no conversation to be had, no points to negotiate, none of that. You either get it, or you don't - there's no in-between. You don't get to play it off as an overreaction," I snapped, trying to keep my emotions at bay, even though I really felt like bursting into tears. "Either my feelings matter more to you than some other bitch or they don't. And my feeling is that your disrespectful ass ex can't be in your face, and you can't be in hers. If that's a sticking point for you, then... We can leave this where it is."

"That's what you wanna do?" He asked, those lights still reflecting off his skin, making the whole thing feel so much more urgent. "Leave it where it is?"

"It seems like what *you* want. Like her being in your life is the more important thing."

"It's not."

"You sure?"

"I'm positive," he said, not dropping his gaze from mine. "Now... Go pack your bag."

chapter twelve

THE WALK TO TRISTAN'S PLACE WAS QUIET.

And short.

It turned out, he only lived about a block and a half away from me, but I'd never been before.

If the progress of our relationship hadn't been so abruptly interrupted by the whole thing with Nya...things would probably be different.

But here I was now, taking in the predictable blacks, grays, wood tones of his space.

"Hey," he said, coming up behind me after he'd put my bag - which he'd insisted on carrying - and his own stuff down. "Seriously... Are you okay?"

"Of course. Whoever it was, they ran. They didn't touch me," I explained, stepping back to give us some distance.

Still.

"I'm not talking about just physically," he countered, pushing his hands into his pockets. "I mean...waking up to somebody busting in your shit... That's not scary to you?"

I blinked.

Had I been *scared*?

Or was it more...resolute?

I had a survival instinct, sure, but fear?

Well, it wasn't really in my makeup to fear a moment I'd been expecting would come.

There had to only be so long that I could live this "new" life without paying anything for it. There, eventually, had to be some sort of reckoning.

Maybe this was it.

"I wasn't scared," I answered him, once I'd thought through it. "I was armed."

Tristan's eyes went wide. "Armed? Like with a weapon?"

"What else would I be referring to, Tristan? My sparkling wit?"

"Keep the attitude, I'm just concerned about you."

"Don't be - I can protect myself."

"It's not about what you *can* do, I'm talking to you, damn."

I blew out a sigh, shaking my head. Maybe I *was* being a little testy, but I was also fresh off having what should have been my sanctuary violated.

Yeah, I was a little tense.

"What am I doing here?" I asked out loud, even though I wasn't really asking him, and the question wasn't even about him.

Not completely.

"Because it makes me feel better," Tristan answered earnestly, not understanding that I meant... *here*.

In this neighborhood, in this country, in... this life.

"Somebody broke into your place, you said they *waited for you*? Yeah, I feel better with you here, not there. Is something wrong with that?"

"Why do you care?"

"Why do I care? Look, I get it, the thing with Nya pissed you off. You're still pissed. I can take that. But you acting like I shouldn't - or don't - give a damn about your wellbeing... it's petty."

"Maybe it's petty, but that doesn't mean it's not valid for me to wonder *why*. I can clearly tell you what I like about you, Tristan. You're charming, and funny, and pretty much a good guy. Maybe a great one. You're handsome, and you're talented, and you're a good father. What can you say about me? Other than fine, and mysterious? You're only interested because I'm a puzzle to figure out, and as soon as I stepped out of place, you made it clear your priority was some other bitch. And now, you wanna swoop in on your white horse for a rescue. But I'm not a goddamn princess trapped in a tower. I'm the bitch they send for the princess' throat. So forgive me if I'm a little stressed, and not that receptive to... whatever this is."

Once I was done with my rant, Tristan said nothing, just stared at me for a long while before he shook his head.

"You know.....," he said, after letting out a dry laugh. "You're right, actually. I *do* like that you're a puzzle to figure out. Am I wrong for that? For being attracted to the fact that you put your mind to something and decided to go for it? For admiring your commitment to rebuilding your life, after whatever it was that you went through? For - yes - finding you gorgeous, for... wanting to be inside you? For - *God forbid* - wanting to get to know you?"

"Oh, here you go with the charm, and the words—"

"And here *you* go with the deflecting," Tristan grunted. "You know what I think? I think the reason you get so fucking reticent about me trying to know you, why it's so strange to you that I might like your ass, is because *you* haven't figured *you* out."

"Oh *really*?"

"Yes really," he nodded. "You don't want me to get too close because you're afraid I might solve that damn puzzle. Hell, it's probably why you flipped about Nya - pushing me away."

"Oh don't you fucking dare. *Don't you fucking dare*," I hissed, moving up to him to jab his chest. "You were in the wrong, *period*, you're not about to-"

"You're right! You're right," he admitted, throwing his hands up. "I don't... I don't even know why I... I'm sorry."

"You said it because niggas can't help themselves, always looking for an out for their bullshit. You can't accept that you were wrong."

"I can," he said, putting a hand to his chest. "I was. I *am* wrong. And I'm sorry. For trying to deflect, and for the fact that it even happened. You're right - I *did* need to check Nya, and... we really *aren't* "friends" like that, to be honest. But I'm right too," he pressed, raising his shoulders. "You're pushing me away, and I wish you wouldn't. I fucked up. I'll own that, T."

"So that makes it okay?"

"If it doesn't, can you tell me what will?" he asked. "I'm not stuck on... one certain way of doing shit. Or... I'm not *trying* to be."

"I don't know what you need to do to make it up, I just know... you hurt my fucking feelings.," I admitted. Which... wasn't easy. But if we were putting it all out there, there was no use pretending it was something else.

"I'm sorry."

His response came quick, but... he meant it.

Still, I shook my head. "Do you even *really* understand why?"

"I do. I made it seem like Nya's presence weighed more than yours, which isn't true. And when you pointed it out... I made it seem like you were the one who was wrong. Instead of owning my shit."

I nodded. "Yeah. My question is still *why?* What the fuck is so special about her?"

Tristan pushed out a sigh. "I guess... familiarity. Consistency.

I have a hard time with... change, I guess. Unless it's change I directly initiated."

"Like pursuing a new woman, even though you're still connected to your ex?"

"We both know I wasn't thinking that far ahead, don't we?"

I didn't *want* to laugh at that, but... I did. "Yeah. We do. The thing is ... we have a chance to correct this now, and decide what, ultimately, we actually want."

"What I *want* is to be good with you."

"We can be *good* without being *together*," I countered.

"Is what you want?"

"I could live with it."

"That's not what I asked you. T, you're the one not being clear, not really saying anything here," Tristan said, raising his shoulders. "I'm not uncertain, or confused, and I'm not too stubborn to say I choose *your* presence in my life over hers, especially since... once *I* really thought about what you said – about what really constituted a friend..."

"I was right, wasn't I?"

When he nodded, I took no joy in that.

Okay, maybe a little.

Fine, a lot.

But I'd stepped into enough interpersonal relationship roles to act them out that I knew this stuff forwards and back. My real-life experience may have been lacking, but I knew the workings inside out, and could recognize what I saw in front of me.

All my problems came when it was time to stop acting, and do it all for real.

"I'm not interested in beefing with you," he said, pulling me from my musings. "And maybe there wouldn't be any hard feelings on your end, you'd "deal", whatever... I'm not interested in that."

"What *are* you interested in?"

"The same thing I've *been* interested in. Since that first night at Urban Grind."

I raised an eyebrow. "Okay... and what's that?"

"You," he answered, simply. "There's *something* here, waiting for us to dig in and discover it. I'm drawn to you, like a fucking magnet. And I know exactly how corny and cliché that sounds, but whatever, I'll take it. I'll be that. But I'll also be all up in your face, until you convince me otherwise," he chuckled, slipping his arms around me to pull me into his body.

I didn't resist it.

Didn't *want* to resist it.

For as much as my feelings had been hurt, as angry as I'd been... I knew it was probably time to let it go. I had no reason to not take him at his word, to give him the chance to prove he really understood what the problem was, and act accordingly.

I wasn't exact, quite, *all the way* ready for that.

"I hope you talked to her. Cause I'ma hurt her feelings if I do it."

"Maybe more than her feelings – you know the only reason she didn't press charges is because none of us saw anything, right?"

I laughed. "At least four of you saw *everything*."

"Nah, nobody saw it," he said, shrugging, and this time... I caught what he was saying. "But anyway...yeah, I talked to her. And she wasn't happy about it, but whatever. Exchanging ink work for loc retwists wasn't really a fair trade anyway."

"No, it wasn't," I agreed, with a deep sigh that shifted the air between us again.

Now I was ready to move on.

"I need to get in the shower, and get to bed. You joining me?"

I bit down on my lip, considering his offer.

It *had* been like two weeks since he'd finally given up the draws, and the memory of it was imprinted in my mind.

Vividly.

And he certainly was making it sound very appealing, with his hands at my waist drawing me toward him, but...

"I think I need a few minutes. So I'm gonna pass," I told him.

He nodded. "Okay. We're good?"

"We're good."

We were.

Really.

He showed me to his room and then disappeared into the attached bathroom – a few seconds later, I heard the shower come on.

It wasn't until then that I could really... *breathe.*

Hours ago, I'd been snatched from sleep by the awareness that something was wrong, and I'd been on a rollercoaster since then. The heightened adrenaline, the anger, and now the confusing ass feelings Tristan brought up...

I needed some quiet.

So I took it.

Not thinking about the overwhelming flow of emotion it would bring about.

One moment I was seated on the edge of Tristan's bed, almost too distracted for further musings about it being my first time seeing it. The next, my chest was heaving, cheeks burning as I dropped my face into my hands, breaking into unexpected sobs.

Tears I'd been fighting for a long ass time.

Reinvention was hard.

It was hard, and confusing, and frustrating, and... painful.

Yes, it was also gratifying, and enlightening, and wonderful, but when it was mixed up with everything else, it all felt like too much.

This was *too much.*

I couldn't keep fighting it.

So I cried, until my throat was aching and my eyes stung and my head was throbbing, but the tears kept coming and coming – I couldn't stop.

Then Tristan's arms were around me.

I wasn't expecting it, and didn't know I needed it until it was happening, but I was so fucking grateful. He was something tangible I could tether myself to, sinking against his shirtless, still-damp chest to calm myself.

He said... *nothing.*

Which was exactly what I needed.

Just the silence, the warmth of his body, the comfort of his arms, the soothing familiarity of his scent, his presence... just *him.*

It felt like a long time before I was able to calm myself enough to lift my head, dragging my puffy eyes open to look Tristan in the face.

"Tell me what's going on?" he said, posing it as a question even though it was clearly an imperative.

I shook my head. "It's just... a lot."

"Because of me. And the break in?"

"Some of both. Plus some other stuff."

"Stuff like...?" he cupped my face in his hands, wiping my cheeks dry with his thumbs before coaxing my gaze to his. "I know you're my mystery woman, but you don't have to keep everything so close to the vest."

I let out a sigh. "I actually kinda do," I said.

"Because of your past life... whatever it is you're rebuilding from."

"Pretty much."

"So... Kiara was right then?" he asked, in a teasing tone. "You really are an assassin... *the girl they send for the princess' throat,* huh? Or will you have to kill me if you tell me?"

I sniffed, shaking my head again. "No, I wouldn't have to kill you. I just... I don't want to be defined by what I've left behind. Even though it's... a pretty defining thing."

"I get that," he nodded. "You're not the sum of the things you've done, and all that."

"Exactly. And I mean... I understand if that's a dealbreaker for you – if it's important to you to know everything about me – about my past. I can't give you that. I *can't*," I repeated, trying my best to not give into a fresh wave of tears. "And if we're going to do this – be together - I need to know that... it doesn't really matter. This chapter of my life isn't – *can't be* - about what I used to do, who I used to be. The real story is who I am now. Who I'm going to become."

"And that is *completely* fine with me," Tristan assured, bringing his lips to mine in a soft press that made everything feel wondrously right with the world.

Obviously I knew it took more than a kiss, more than a conversation, more than this moment, but... for now, at least... I'd happily take it.

And I'd take all the other kisses he offered – I'd take them greedily, needing something else to focus on. I'd take off the towel wrapped around Tristan's waist, making him laugh.

But then he pushed me down on the bed, and there was nothing funny anymore.

He stripped me out of my clothes and dropped his head between my legs, propping my thighs over his shoulders. I didn't need to watch – I let my head fall back, letting my tired eyes rest as Tristan demanded the last of whatever energy my tired body had left, forcing it to expend itself in pursuit of sweet bliss.

I bucked against his mouth, my hips jerking, back arching away from the bed as he devoured me. My fingers dug into the soft fabric of his comforter, my only hold on anything that wasn't pure pleasure as he kept on, and on, until I couldn't help screaming his name, hoarse and all.

And then he was on top of me.

Then inside me.

Filling me up, and making me forget everything except how good this felt, growling in my ear about how good it was for him, too.

I'd missed him.

Missed this.

Which probably should've scared me more than it did, considering how quickly things had changed between us after the first time we were intimate.

I wasn't afraid.

This – Tristan inside me – felt righter than many things over the time since the disbanding of the *Garden*.

Once we were done, I *did* end up in the shower with Tristan – apparently he'd heard me crying, and had cut his earlier one short. Afterwards, he insisted I join him for a quick bite, and then we went to bed.

He fell asleep fast, with an arm draped around me.

As for me… I had a little more to think about.

I wasn't going to run from… whatever this was.

Not Tristan, not the shop, not any of things that might come along with this new life I was making for myself.

I didn't know yet who had violated the safety of the shop, but not even *that* was going to scare me off.

At least… not without a fight.

And I wasn't particularly known for losing those.

chapter thirteen

SOMETHING WAS WRONG.

It woke me from my sleep, again, only this time, I had Tristan in bed beside me.

And *he* was the "something wrong".

Instead of his typical, peaceful state, his shoulders were tense. He was facing away from me, but I didn't have to see his lips – I could hear his pained, unintelligible murmurs, knew his face was likely pulled into a frown, eyes still closed.

I said nothing, but put a hand against his bare shoulder, gently running my fingers over the *Heights* tattoo there. City buildings forming a circle, with *The Heights* scripted in the middle. He wasn't the only one who had it, but he'd designed it – one of several designs the shop offered free to anyone who wanted it. Anyone who lived in the neighborhood, that is.

I squeezed his shoulder – not to wake him up, but more like... making sure he knew, even subconsciously, that he wasn't alone.

If that mattered, or helped.

Maybe.

I immediately felt the difference when he woke up, but I

didn't move my hand. I waited for him to fully awake, turning to face me with a groggy, confused expression.

"You wanna talk about it?" I asked.

He blinked a few times, pushing his locs back from his face like he was considering it before finally, he shook his head. "Nah. I don't want to be defined by what I left behind."

I smirked over his recycling of my own words as he moved in closer to me under the covers, the feeling of his skin reminding me that neither of us had *anything* on. It struck me that he might've been trying to distract me so I wouldn't press, but he didn't have to – for one, because I wouldn't dare not give him the same space I wanted for myself, from my past. Secondly... I felt like I could pretty much guess what was bothering him – what stayed at the fringes of his mind. From what Kiara described, Tristan had seen combat, which could fuck up anybody. My experience – my past – was different enough from his, yes, but... the death, the vigilance, the necessary grit... it all paralleled.

Wanting to let it stay where it was, instead of sullying the goodness and light that could be ahead of us?

That was something we had in common.

"What are your plans for today? What you got going on?" he asked, very casually, like he wasn't gripping a handful of my ass as he spoke.

Like his dick wasn't hard and distracting against my pelvis.

"Well, Anika recommended a stylist to me, so I'm going to get a much-needed trim, and deep conditioner, all that," I told him, snaking a hand between us. "And then I'm gonna make some candles. You?"

His eyes closed, a moan slipping from his throat as my fingers closed around his dick. "Uh... shit. Um. My mother is coming up, gonna stay a few days – in a hotel. Kiara's birthday is this coming weekend, remember? We're going get the grill going at the park, a couple deep fryers..."

"Yes, I remember you mentioning it."

"Right. So you'll be there?"

My eyes went wide and my hand stopped, putting immediate brakes on the slow stroking motion I'd started. "What?"

His lids lifted, gaze meeting mine. "Did I say something confusing?"

"Confusing, no. Surprising, yes."

"It's surprising that because you're in my life, I would want you to be part of celebrating my child?"

"I just... didn't think we were *there* yet."

Tristan's lips curved into a smile. "You've met Kiara. She likes you – spy conspiracy theory and all. I don't understand what exactly we'd be waiting on."

I started to object, but... I really couldn't find a rebuttal for that. He was right – we'd already met, however inadvertently. Not to mention the whole *slice a nigga in the street* incident I was still figuring out who I needed to talk to about.

"Your mother, though," I said. "And presumably Von is gonna be there – she hates me."

"She definitely doesn't," Tristan laughed. "And my mother will *love* you."

"And if she doesn't?"

"Better to know now than later, right?"

"What?!"

"Baby, listen," he grabbed my chin. "I know it sounds like a lot. And honestly, maybe this *is* really soon. But... I thought you weren't pussy?"

"Did you forget your dick is my hand?"

"Not at all. I'm hoping you decide to climb on and teach me a lesson."

Instead, I squeezed him a little too hard.

"It's not funny."

"I'm not laughing," he countered, still cringing.

I stared at him for a long moment, then pumped my hand again. "Do I need to bring anything?"

"Just yourself. And your sparkling personality."

"Uh huh." I hissed as he slipped a hand between my legs, his attention focused on my sensitive clit.

"So you'll be there?"

A moan rumbled in my throat as he pushed those fingers further – pushed them into me.

"Yes."

ALICIA INSISTED ON AN ALARM SYSTEM.

That had been her biggest thing, when I talked to her that morning that followed the break-in.

She was fine with the supposition that this was a random crime or even that I was targeted - for being such a lovely addition to the neighborhood, not for my past.

But still.

She wanted me to get an alarm system at least, just in case.

"Normalcy makes you rusty," she'd said, meaning it as a teasing thing, but it was rooted in truth. I wasn't training like I used to - I wasn't training at all. Wasn't being challenged in the ways in which I'd grown accustomed.

I was eating too much macaroni and cheese at Pot Liquor, doing too much hanging out and laughing with Anika and Jules, too much texting with Dacia and Pen.

I was gonna open the candle shop. Willow handled most of the paperwork for that, but there was still a need to make a shit ton of candles.

Another deep distraction.

And then - worst? - of all... I was incredibly, disgustingly wrapped up in Tristan.

And I was... happy.

You'd be even happier if you get your ass to that hair appointment..

Oh shit.

Yes.

I was already dressed and ready to go, just had to stop musing about the meaning of life long enough to actually set the alarm on the shop and leave. I was still getting used to it, but it was simple enough.

On the other side of the door, I took a step back, admiring the logo printed on the new - *expensive* - glass. It was simple, but it was mine, and made me feel... solid.

Yeah.

"Tempest Lane?"

The sound of my name made me turn around, to see two cops approaching me. Instantly, my shoulders tensed, but I put on a neutral face.

"Yes?"

It was a quick conversation.

Apparently, my little creep friend - the one who'd grabbed me at Urban Grind, harassed Kiara, etc. - was a fucking criminal all around. He'd been picked up for something else, and immediately started screaming about how *"That candle shop bitch deserved what she got, that bitch cut me!"*

Did I know anything about him being cut?

No, officer, of course not. That's crazy!

He'd say anything to get himself out of trouble, right?

They bought it. And they moved on from there, assuring me that he wouldn't be seeing the streets of the neighborhood anytime soon, which I guess was supposed to give me some of comfort.

Not really.

Really I wanted them to go away, cause their asses made me nervous too.

It felt... too easy.

Not that I *wanted* to be looking over my shoulder for whoever had broken into the shop, but in the list of possibilities for who might've been behind that break-in, ol' boy had been low to me.

Or maybe I was overthinking it... expecting the worst.

Anyway.

I was definitely late for my appointment now, but the stylist was cool, brushing off my apology with a wave when I did arrive.

"My last client *just* walked out of here like two minutes ago, so you're fine," she insisted, ushering me into her chair. "Otherwise, I'd be feeling bad for having you waiting. Let's get you started today."

I'd forgotten what it felt like to have someone else doing this stuff for me.

In the *Garden*, it had been standard – professional haircare, skincare, the works. We learned the basics of doing it all ourselves if necessary, but when a certain level of aesthetics was a requirement of the business model, you mostly left it to the experts.

Since it all fell apart, I'd been doing it myself.

Now, it was amazing to have skilled hands doing the shampooing, detangling, deep conditioning, all that. Beyond the actual haircare, the salon itself was a soothing environment, rich and vibrant with all its smells and loud voices and the hum of the dryers and laughter.

"You have such nice *strong* hair," Andrea – my stylist – complimented as she combed through my tresses, preparing for my blowout. "I can tell you've been taking good care of it."

"*That's all her hair*?!"

I rolled my eyes at the sound of Nya's voice. She'd been

staring a hole in the side of my head since she came in, but I'd opted for simply ignoring her.

"You watched me shampoo her and all that – you *know* it's her hair," Andrea replied, sounding annoyed.

At the next station, Nya sucked her teeth, clearly bored while her client was under the dryer. "I'm just saying, it was looking like some kinda homemade extensions the way she was walking around here looking. My bad."

"Find some damn business."

I kept my lips shut, letting the conversation remain between Andrea and Nya. I'd had a great morning with Tristan, and no interest in letting her rile me.

"I've got plenty of business," Nya snapped. "When I finish up my client, I may go down to the tattoo shop to see about some new ink. I've gotta find a new artist."

Andrea picked up her dryer, but didn't turn it on yet. "Why do you need a new artist? Tristan finally get sick of your ass?"

"Tristan could never get sick of *this* ass," she giggled. "His new bitch didn't want him around me. That's so sad. To not be enough to keep a man, so you've gotta worry about him with other women."

Andrea had flipped the dryer on while Nya was talking, but switched it back off to laugh. "Um... obviously if he has a "new bitch" you couldn't *keep* him either, so..."

"Nah I've moved on," Nya stammered. "We were just friends... with benefits, of course. But that girl is *so* crazy insecure, and jealous of me."

Okay.

Now *that* was my last fucking straw.

"Girl jealous of *what,* exactly?" I snapped, and Andrea's mouth dropped open as I turned to face Nya in the chair. "There is not shit about you or your sad ass existence to envy, and I really wish you'd stop it."

Nya smirked, but had enough good sense to ease back. "You're talking shit like I didn't have you shook about your man."

"*You* didn't have me "shook" about a thing where Tristan is concerned. I took my issue with him *to* him. And I took my issue with you, *to you*. Do I need to remind you what my hands feel like around your neck, bitch?"

"I'd rather remember Tristan's."

"And that's all it'll ever be for you – a memory," I shot back.

"If you were so sure of that, you wouldn't have been bothered by us being friends. Like I said – *insecure*."

I shrugged. "You call it insecurity, I call it a demand that the boundaries of our relationship are well-defined and respected. Either way, *you're* looking like a fucking fool, arguing with a woman who cares nothing about you over a man who doesn't want you. Only one of us is going out sad in this situation, dear," I smiled, then turned back to Andrea. "Can we...?"

"Of course," Andrea chirped, beaming. "Let's get you together with a fresh style for *your* man to fuck up."

If Nya had anything else to say, I didn't hear it.

Really.

I tuned her completely out, losing myself in the hum of the dryer and my own thoughts – beating myself up for responding to her bullshit at all.

It was another thing I was losing – the discipline.

Getting provoked by *words*?

Never.

Not before.

Between everything – good and bad – with Tristan, these interactions with Kiara and other people in the neighborhood, this thing with Nya... shit.

I'd *never* been so reactionary and emotional and... *human*.

I stopped beating myself up over it when I thought about it like that.

For better or worse, this was what I'd wanted.

And really... it wasn't so bad.

I scheduled a follow-up with Andrea in two weeks and then went on my way, stopping by Urban Grind for my brown sugar cinnamon iced latte first. I'd given myself the lofty goal of opening the shop in the next few weeks, so I had candles and labels to make.

As I was standing in line for my drink, I glanced out the window to look across the street. To my surprise, there was a woman standing there, peering up at the *Wax Poetic* logo, and then into the store. It didn't seem like a big deal, so I went about my business, but once I'd gotten my drink and was headed out, the woman was still there.

That was a little strange.

My phone started ringing, so I pulled it out, smiling when I saw Dacia's name on the screen. Besides the fact that being on the phone was a great cover, I hadn't actually *spoken* to her in a while.

"Hello?" I answered, my eyes still on the stranger in front of my shop as I crossed the street.

"Hey, where are you?" Dacia asked, on the other end of the line, her voice creating a weird echo... that didn't seem so weird at all when the "stranger" finally turned so I could see her profile.

"*Dosh!*" I yelled, my outburst startling her for a moment until she turned to see me rushing in her direction. I ended the call, dropping the phone into my pocket as I opted to hug her in real life instead of bothering with the phone. "What are you doing here?!"

She laughed, hugging me back with the same excited energy I'd given her. "I just... needed a change of scenery, and I wanted to see the shop, and wanted to see *you*. So here I am."

Yes, indeed, she was.

Looking *so much* healthier than the last time I saw her.

There wasn't a rose among us who'd escaped the *Garden* with no trauma, but Dacia had gone through... even more. She was managing well enough – as well as could be expected – but the last time I'd seen her in person, it was so evident in her eyes.

Now, her pretty brown eyes were clear and happy, and she'd let go of the baggy clothes and simple slicked-back ponytail she'd been using as armor. *No wonder I hadn't recognized her.* She was, now, as I remembered her from the *Garden*, when she'd been utilized to teach the petals their hair and makeup.

Face done, curls big and free, a cute outfit.

Her natural setpoint.

"Well, come in," I insisted, balancing my cup in the bend of my arm so I could unlock the door.

She squealed when she stepped in, looking around as I tended to the alarm. "So you were really not messing around when you said you were doing this, huh?"

"I was really not."

I grinned as she picked up one of the candles, taking the top off to bring it to her nose. "Oooh, this smells good," she gushed, turning it to look at the label. "*Brown Sugar Cinnamon Latte,*" she read, then looked at me. "Is that what's in the cup?"

"Yup. Today at least," I amended, laughing. "I've been discovering new *favorites* on a weekly basis, so I've done scents to match several."

"Is that gonna be your *thing*? All coffeehouse scents?"

"Nah." I picked up a different one, handing it to her. "My *thing* is gonna be... stuff I love."

She lifted an eyebrow at me as she inhaled the one I'd given her, then looked to see the label – it didn't have one. "Temp, this... smells like a man. So you're in love now?"

"With *him*? No. I mean... I don't know. It's way too soon to know something like that," I stammered. "But I *definitely* love the way he smells. That's without question."

I took the candle from her to breathe it in again, pleased that I'd been able to capture that pleasing signature cedar and citrus Tristan seemed to carry with him.

"Why doesn't it have a label?" Dacia asked, and I shrugged.

"I haven't come up with the name for it yet."

She smirked. "Just call it... *Tristan*," she teased, putting this breathy gasp of air with it that made me laugh. "Seriously – I want to meet his ass."

"I think I can make that happen. We can—"

"Knock-knock!"

I heard, at the same time as the bell over the door sounded, signaling that someone had come in. We looked up to see Carlos from next door standing there, hands propped on his hips.

"Ms. Ma'am, I know you're *not* gonna not introduce me to your lil' friend. I was sitting right outside, and you were too busy embracing like reunited lovers to even see me on the balcony, but I was *there*." He lifted his head, eyes narrowed. "*Are you reunited lovers?*"

I laughed, shaking my head. "We're not."

"Ugh. Boring," he declared, waving me off as he sauntered up to where we stood. "I'm Carlos, beautiful," he said, offering his hand. "And you are?"

"Dacia Pelletier," she answered, accepting his hand. "Temp's friend."

Carlos' eyes went wide. "Did you say *Pelletier?*"

"Yes..."

"As in... *Adam Pelletier?*"

Instantly, Dacia tensed. "Yes."

"Oh honey. Come with me," he said, grabbing her by the hand before either of us could really react to it.

I sprang forward, ready to intervene, but Dacia didn't snatch away. I didn't know if she was too stunned or what, but I restrained myself, simply following as Carlos pulled her out of my storefront to take her next door, into Keem's showroom where he was working with a customer.

Keem looked up, surprised, but went back to his client while Carlos led us to a rack of fur coats. "I've got Adam Pelletier's kinfolk here with the vintage Pelletier furs – I gotta get a pic-flick-flick of this, where is my phone?"

"There are *Pelletier* furs?" Dacia asked, eyes wide as she reached out to skim the luxury pieces with her hands.

"Like these are pieces your dad made? From his brand?" I asked, and Dacia nodded, a big smile spreading over her face.

"It's been really hard to find any of the original animal fur pieces. I mean, even the faux fur ones with this label are scarce, but these *minks*… these are rare. Real treasures."

"And they're yours, my dear," Keem declared in his deep baritone as he walked up. Apparently, he'd sent his client off, and was ready to join the conversation. "Carlos says you're a relative?"

"I'm his daughter. One of his daughters," she corrected, obviously thinking of her older sister, Alicia. "How much do you want for them?"

Carlos and Keem *both* shot her a look like she was crazy. "Not a dime," Keem said. "The *colonizer* I got these from was very pleased to let me know these came from the family collection, *pillaged* after the home invasion that took your father's life, and subjected you girls to whatever you went through after that. He thought it would raise the price."

"But after *I* read his alabaster ass out from commencement to conclusion, he found himself some damn sense," Carlos added.

"So what we're saying is, we can't accept your money – they aren't even for sale, they're on display. Until now, when we have the absolute *honor* of returning what's rightfully yours and your sister's." Keem took Dacia by the hands, squeezing them together. "*Please.*"

I wasn't sure Dacia *could* answer.

Her eyes were glossy with unshed tears, and I could feel the heaviness coming off her, to the point that I thought I should probably get her out of there.

As harmlessly as they'd obviously meant this little reunion with her past... it had to be, still... triggering.

"Thank you," she finally spoke, nodding as those tears started dripping down her face. "I wasn't... I wasn't expecting something like this, like... *at all,*" she laughed, turning to me. "Who knew?"

"Definitely not me," I laughed, stepping up to put an arm around her.

We worked out some logistics for getting the coats, stoles, and whatever else, back to her place in Vegas, then I took her back next door. She had a hotel room, but I kept her in my apartment to regroup from the unexpected emotion of the encounter with Carlos and Keem. Well... I left her upstairs, and went down to the workshop to give her some privacy while she called Alicia to share the news.

When she was done, she came looking for me, grinning when she saw me pouring candles. "I can't get over this – you have gone from one of *the* most formidable roses I've ever met to... *candlemaker*. What is even happening here?"

"We all need an outlet, don't judge me," I laughed.

"No judgement here," she said, taking a seat. "Writing has been mine, at the advice of my therapist, who doesn't even know quite how bad it all is."

"Like journaling or something?"

She shook her head. "Like a book. *Books*. I'm going to get it all out. You know... a year or so ago, I wrote some of it out, and put it on the internet? The rose tattoos and all. I took it down, because that was dumb."

"Bitch. You're serious?"

She chuckled. "Yeah, I really did that."

"I *know* you did, because Tristan's *kid* read it," I yelled. "I didn't know it was *you* who would do something so... so..."

"Fucking stupid? Yeah," Dacia nodded. "It was when everything first happened, and I was so... lost. Angry at everybody. Confused. Scared. It felt like taking my power back, until I thought about how it might hurt other roses. I'm sorry."

"You don't have to be sorry," I told her, brushing off the apology. "I played it off well enough, but she still believes it. I didn't say anything to you or Alicia or Pen because I... honestly I figured it was one of us, trying to figure shit out. But it being *you* is ... wild. You show up and all the coincidences start raining in."

Dacia smiled. "Yeah well... I've got one more for you."

"What's that?" I asked, raising an eyebrow. "I don't know if I can take anymore."

"This one might be pretty simple... maybe?"

I put down my pouring vessel to prop my hands on my hips. "Girl spill it."

"I want to get my rose covered."

Any annoyance I'd been feeling dissipated. "Oh! Really?"

More than once, she and Alicia had both been vocal about not wanting theirs removed or covered, for whatever their personal reasons were. So it was surprising to hear this now.

"Yeah. I just... I feel like I've made so many strides, towards getting to a place of normalcy. Finally feeling human again. And then... I look in the mirror, and all the horror and ugliness comes screaming back. I don't want that anymore."

I nodded, knowing *exactly* what she meant. That same feeling had plagued me for a long, long time before I finally took that plunge, and I hadn't looked back.

The rose never crossed my mind anymore, not unbidden.

"You're right," I told her, wiping my hands. "That one *is* simple. You need a tattoo, and you want to meet Tristan, right?"

She smiled. "Right."

"Cool. I think I know a way to get both of those covered."

It didn't take much.

Just a quick text to Tristan, who happened to have a short opening where he could squeeze in a favor for me. He *did* give me a look when Dacia showed him the rose in the same place as mine, nearly identical except for the color.

But he didn't comment any further.

He turned it a fiery phoenix for her.

Not as much detail as mine since he'd worked her in, but still beautiful, and still enough to meet the desired goal.

One less woman defined by a mark she hadn't chosen.

We thanked him, helped clean up before his next client, and then left, feeling good for different reasons.

Dacia was excited about her tattoo, rightfully so.

And I... was excited for her.

It was new to me – all of this. Having friends to be happy to reunite with, friends I wanted to call in favors for.

Having a friend – a *lover* – who could carry that favor out.

Happily.

This new, full life was so different from a few months ago.

And I wanted *every* moment of it.

chapter fourteen

"So you're telling me you've never seen *any* of them?" Tristan pressed, in full disbelief of my lack of knowledge on a whole host of classic Black movies. Between age and very-fucked-up experience, they'd just never been on my radar. Most of my movie trivia knowledge came from vast pop-culture lists I'd needed to study for conversation purposes, not actual viewing experience.

"Asking a third time won't change the answer, sir," I told him over the phone, as I pressed the label to the candle I'd finally named – a name he hadn't yet seen. I wasn't sure how *Tristan* was going to react to the *Neighborhood Hottie* scent, but Dacia, Jules, and Anika all loved it, so I was pretty confident it would be a hit.

"Tell me you're willing to let me change your life," he said, making my eyebrows shoot up.

"Huh?"

"We've gotta institute a weekly movie date or something, I can't have you out with me in the *Heights* not catching the references and shit."

"*Oh*," I laughed. "Yeah, I'd be into that," I told him, grabbing the backing sheets from the pile of labels I'd just finished applying. I'd been a candle-making machine the last few days, and almost had the minimum stock for the shop ready.

"You sure? You're not one of those people who don't like movies at all, are you?"

Hm.

I... actually had no idea.

But for the purposes of this conversation, I assured him that I was not, knowing that even if I discovered I *hated* movies, I would enjoy the time spent with *him*.

... and his mouth.

... and his dick.

"When do you wanna start?" I asked, already plotting how little attention I would be giving the TV at all. "I know you have Kiara tonight, and then the party is tomorrow, but... the day after that?"

He chuckled. "Damn, you're excited about this, huh?"

"Very."

"Yeah, the day after should be fine," he agreed. "Your place or mine?"

"Well... considering the fact that I don't have a TV..."

"Oh shit, that's right," he groaned. "I keep meaning to fix that."

"It's not a thing to *fix*," I laughed. "You're not fucking up my minimalist aesthetic so you can watch... whatever niggas watch while they're laid up at their woman's house."

"So you're claiming me now? That's whassup."

"When was I not claiming you?"

"Kiara said *you* said, *'I'm not your daddy's girlfriend'*."

I cringed. "Well, at the time I wasn't. We hadn't talked things out yet."

"Only because you wouldn't talk to me."

"And when I *did* talk to you, you were still trying to blame your fuck up on everything but yourself, so I can't imagine the conversation would've been productive if it happened any sooner."

Tristan let out a heavy sigh. "That's a pretty fair point I guess. She also told me you intervened with some motherfuckers who were harassing her? Why didn't you tell me that?"

"Your daughter was afraid you'd do something to land yourself in jail. And frankly, I was too," I admitted. "But really, I was trying to figure out the right way to approach it, then the ringleader wound up getting arrested for something else. *Including* breaking into the shop."

"I'll see him when he gets out. But in the meantime... thank you for being on Kiara's team, even though me and you were beefing."

"You don't have to thank me for that," I told him, staring at the pile of recycling that stood between me and a pristine workshop going into the weekend. "I wasn't about to stand by while they harassed her."

"But you could've. So be ready to hear about it from Von too, tomorrow. She doesn't play about her baby girl, so that got you a *lot* of points with her."

"Did I *need* points with her?"

"No, but it doesn't hurt."

"Because it matters to you what she thinks of me."

"Is that a bad thing?"

"It would be a bad thing if you *didn't* care what she thought of me," I answered. "She's the mother of your child, and I've never heard you say a bad thing about her. She's gonna be in your life, and *I'm* going to be in your life, so... it's important that we can all get along."

"I agree. I don't think that's going to be an issue, since like I said – she likes you."

"She doesn't know me."

"She likes what she knows *of you*."

I shook my head. "I... guess we'll see tomorrow."

"We definitely will," he said. "Ay, did you ever eat anything for dinner? You didn't mention it again..."

Shit.

I had declined Tristan's offer earlier in the evening to have something delivered with the promise I would take care of myself. Truthfully, I'd gotten too distracted with work, and forgot.

So... no.

I had *not* had dinner.

"Baby, come *on*," he scolded. "You keep getting all wrapped up in those candles, you're gonna end up passing out. Breathing in all those fumes without eating..."

"Fumes?" I laughed. "That's a stretch."

"After you've complained about being lightheaded from being in your workroom for hours and hours? I don't think so."

"Who asked you anyway?"

"*I* asked me," he chuckled. "And I'm gonna ask again, do you need me to send you something?"

"No, I've got it – for real this time," I assured. "I'm gonna take this recycling out back, then I'm done in the workshop for the day, and I can eat the rest of my big ass salad from lunch."

"You're definitely gonna do that?"

"I swear," I giggled, bending to push the pile of disassembled boxes into a stack that would be easier for me to carry out. "I'll call you back after."

"Aiight. Talk to you in a few."

"Bye."

I slipped the phone into my pocket and gathered the boxes, tucking them under one arm so I could get the door. It was awkward, but I still managed, taking a deep breath of the late spring air as I stepped out.

And immediately regretting it.

The little bit of coolness it used to carry was gone, replaced by the mugginess usually reserved for summer. Because of that, I didn't linger in the semi-darkness, using the glow of the "safety lighting" that lined the back alley to guide me to the bright blue dumpster.

"*One trip down*," I mumbled to myself as I dropped the boxes inside. "*Ah!*" I screamed when I turned around, startled to find someone blocking my path.

Nya.

"Excuse me..." I muttered, stepping around her, but not thinking much of it... until she moved to get *back* in my face.

"I'm really sick of you," she declared, her face pulled into a scowl. "Where the fuck did you even come from, getting in the way?"

I raised an eyebrow. "The feeling is quite mutual, sis. And you're the only one in somebody's way here. *Move*."

"I'm *not* scared of you!" To prove her point, she shoved me backward, wearing a satisfied smirk. It was nothing for me to catch my balance, which I did, but I was so caught off guard by this aggression that it was *all* I did.

Which she thought was funny.

"I see you're not so big and bold now, without an audience. Without Tristan to protect you. Weird ass *bitch*," she screamed, poising herself to shove me again, but that shit wasn't happening.

I hit her twice – two jabs right to the face, then easily swept her legs from under her, sending her tumbling to the ground.

Where she remained, and started crying. "What the fuck is wrong with you?!" she shrieked, making me frown.

"*Me?* Bitch what is wrong with *you?* You're the one sneaking up on people in the dark, attacking. I should shoot your dumb ass!" I told her, pulling the gun I'd started carrying since the break-in from my waistband to prove my point. It was a cutesy little thing, lighter than what I would've used on assignment, but I needed something easy to conceal, so it got the job done.

When I pointed it at her, she screamed, holding her hands up in front of her face.

"I didn't mean to, I swear!" she insisted. "I was cutting through back here to get home, and I saw you, and I ... got so mad. You embarrassed me at my job!"

"You embarrassed *yourself*," I countered, shaking my head. "Nobody told you to start any shit with me – *you* did that."

"So you pull a gun on me?!"

"The gun is because you attacked me, bitch are you really this dense?!" I snapped, annoyed. This girl really had my adrenaline going, for no damn reason. "Get your dumb ass up."

I watched as she scrambled to her feet, grabbing the purse she'd dropped too. For a moment, I believed I'd be able to let her walk away from here with a stern warning to leave me the fuck alone, but as soon as she slipped her hand inside her purse, I knew.

With my safety on, I smacked her across the face with the gun, sending her and the contents of her bag spilling to the ground again as she wailed into the night.

Ignoring her as she held her hands to her face, I scanned the ground around her, my eyes landing on the stun gun she must've been going for.

"That's really wack, you know?" I called out, kicking it away from her. "I should shoot you for real, so I don't have to worry about you coming back to be annoying."

"Let it be, honey."

I looked up to find Keem with his arms crossed, leaning against the atelier's back door, watching us with a solemn look in his eyes. As I watched, he pushed himself off and approached us, bending to help Nya gather her stuff.

"Take your ass on," he told her, pushing her bag into her hands. "Don't lose more than you have to trying to preserve your pride."

She opened her mouth to argue, then must've thought better of it when her gaze fell on me. She grabbed her purse from Keem and scrambled on down the alley while he stepped in my way, blocking me.

"What the fuck was that?" I asked, tucking the gun back in my waistband where it had been. "Her silly ass keeps starting shit with me, and you interrupted me making sure it doesn't happen again."

Keem laughed. "I think she got the message. She's silly. Not a mark."

Not a mark?

I already had my gun back in my grip, raised and aimed for a head shot, safety off, finger on the trigger, by the time he lifted his hands in front of him, gesturing that he meant no harm.

"No weapon necessary - you came onto my turf - not the other way around, remember?"

Since it was late, he was dressed much more casually than I was used to seeing him around his showroom - basketball shorts and a tee shirt. He stepped further into the light, pushing his sleeve up his bicep to show me what was inked there.

A ring of thorns.

"I knew the very first time I saw you," he explained, letting his sleeve back down. "Could tell. At first I thought you were coming for me, but I've been out of the Garden for at least a decade... No reason for anybody to come for me now. So I figured you must've gotten away, somehow. I didn't want to spook you, so I didn't say anything."

"The *Garden* doesn't exist anymore," I told him, and he chuckled.

"As long as you're looking over your shoulder, it does. And you'll always be looking over your shoulder. I still do."

"But you decided I wasn't a threat." I lowered my gun, trying to decide if I was offended by that or not.

He grinned at me. "You're definitely a threat. Just not to me."

"Fair enough," I answered, putting my weapon fully away now. If Keem wanted to kill me, he'd had ample opportunity over these months I'd been right next door. "So... You've been out for a decade?"

"Presumed dead. I'm a ghost, basically. I built myself a new life, but there wasn't any real peace until the *Garden* was eliminated. Thanks to the *Pelletier* sisters."

My eyebrows went up. "So... You knew more than you let on, about Dacia."

"Something like that. Something neither of you needed to know."

"But you're outing yourself now. Why?"

"To keep you from being a murderer."

I frowned. "I wasn't going to *kill* her. I was about to kick her ass. And anyway, you say that as if she would've been the first."

"She would've, right? Since you're not that person anymore. Not a *rose* anymore. That life is gone, behind you. Unless I've mistaken this process of you revamping a candle shop, getting a boyfriend, integrating yourself into the neighborhood..."

"No," I shook my head. "You're right, this is what I wanted, I just—"

"Just nothing," Keem interrupted. "If you don't want to be that girl, don't be. It doesn't mean you have to take any shit, but slicing people on the street and pistol whipping them in alleys doesn't exactly scream *normal girl*."

"They started it."

Keem laughed. "I'm sure they did. But if you've decided what you want to be now, be that. And don't let these peons take you out of your new, permant character. Don't let anyone jeopardize who you're trying to be."

I sucked my teeth. "I already have a mentor, thanks."

"And I'm not trying to put myself in that role - just telling you what I've learned over the years. And the biggest lesson is that... It's okay to let that shit go. I mean, be smart, pay attention, all that. But... live. *Love*. Fully. If somebody is gonna come for you, they will, but in the meantime you may as well enjoy this shit. I sure as hell am."

Without anything more to say, Keem went inside, leaving me standing in dark, mind reeling.

The ultimate conclusion I came to, was that he was right - I wouldn't be able to straddle the fence forever. Not without sacrificing my sanity.

And that was too valuable to put on the line.

I wasn't as far removed as he was, so it would take me some time, but his advice wasn't so different - wasn't *any* different, really, from Alicia's.

To enjoy this life I'd carved out for myself, and not let anything fuck it up.

So... I'd try.

If Nya fucked with me again her ass was mine though.

chapter fifteen

THERE WAS A WHOLE LOT OF *FINE* IN THE HEIGHTS.

Like… a lot of it.

Maybe a little too much.

As I sat in the park, off to myself, observing, my gaze had landed on Tristan and a bunch of other guys, all in varying degrees of shirtlessness, talking a bunch of trash to each other as they played basketball.

It was a sight to fucking behold.

"Girl. *Same.*"

Jules and Anika parked themselves on either side of the bench where I'd been seated alone – prime viewing area for the basketball court, and downwind of the delicious smells from the food.

"Huh?" I asked Anika, and she smirked.

"You're looking at them like you wouldn't mind hopping up to get sweaty too, and I must say… it has crossed my mind as well."

"*Oh*," I laughed, shaking my head. "They are over there looking like good reasons for bad decisions, aren't they?"

"I think we made good decisions," Jules countered, biting down on her lip as Troy fouled the *shit* out of one of the guys I didn't know. "I need Troy to bring some of that aggression back home later. Take it straight to the hole."

Anika giggled. "Yes, Royal, penetrate *me* right up the middle, and go for the money shot."

They both looked at me, waiting for me to round out the whole basketball innuendo thing they had going on, but...

"Sorry," I shrugged. "There's a "facial" joke somewhere I can't quite pull it together."

"It's okay," Jules laughed. "We won't disown you this time."

"I don't have time to keep it going anyway," Anika said as she stood. "Popped through to give birthday wishes to Kiara, but I've gotta get my butt to the coffeehouse for a shift."

"And I've got pictures to take – official event photographer and all," Jules added, gesturing to her camera before she pointed it to where Kiara was standing with her friends, giggling. *They* had their attention on the other court, where a group of teenage boys were occupying the space.

Cute.

That was the kind of thing young girls *should* be doing at thirteen – giggling about cute boys their age. Not... training. I understood that my experience was abnormal, but still. *Seeing* these girls get to be children did my heart a lot of good.

"See ya later Tee!"

I waved to Jules and Anika as they headed off, giving my attention back to my surroundings once they were gone.

Watching.

Just like I'd spent my first few months in the *Heights*, only this time I wasn't tucked away behind my window.

And I didn't feel like I needed to be, either.

"You eat anything for breakfast?"

Von was standing in front of me, tall and regal as ever. Her tone wasn't the friendliest, but it wasn't unkind either, so I decided to entertain her question with a nod.

"Good," she said, taking the seat beside me. "That means you can drink with me."

Before I could object, she'd pushed a cold, half-frosted beer bottle into my hands, and had already lifted an identical one to her lips as I examined the label.

Auntie's House.

"It's not spiked with anything, if that's what you're worried about," she said, mistaking my curiosity for apprehension.

"I didn't think you'd do anything like that," I told her, honestly, lifting the bottle to my mouth to take a sip. "You don't strike me as the sneak-attack type."

"Cheers to that." She twisted her bottle in my direction, and I did the same, tapping the glasses together. "So... I wanted to apologize for how I came at you that day in *grown*. That was my bad. I don't want you to think I'm hung up on Tristan having a girlfriend or anything, it's just that his *last* girlfriend..."

"Oh I've had to put hands on her."

"So you feel me then," Von laughed, shaking her head. "Tristan is a good dude, honestly. He was just really wild for that one. I'm glad he got his shit together."

I took another, longer sip from the surprisingly good beer, taking the moment to consider my words before I spoke. "If that's the case... why aren't you together?"

She didn't answer immediately, which I appreciated. It made me feel like it wasn't rehearsed. "I think that... if he and I weren't involved with other people, maybe we would give it a try, you know? But that's not the case. I know that's likely not the most reassuring thing in the world, but it's honest. Everything you see in Tristan, I see it too. But I found those same things in someone else already, while Tristan was either still growing up, or halfway around the world, or recovering from what being halfway around the world did to him. I didn't mold him, or wait for him, or heal him. Because I deserved love without having to do any of that."

My eyes went wide. "He expected that from you?"

"No, not at all," Von quickly amended. "And I don't mean to imply that he did, I'm just saying… that's why we aren't, and weren't together. Because *he* wasn't together. Now he is. And you get to deal with *that* guy, instead of what he was. He still has his moments. But I guess we all have those, right?" she teased, presumably referring to her rudeness in *grown*. "Again… I'm sorry for spazzing on you. Tristan seems to really like you, and so does Kiara. And she told us what you did for her, when those motherfuckers were bothering her. You protected my baby. So as far as I'm concerned… you're good with me."

I smiled, extending my bottle to her again. "The feeling is mutual."

"We drinkin' over here?!"

My grin grew even bigger as I recognized Tristan's mother – it wasn't hard, considering she was wearing the same *"unfuckwittable"* tee shirt from that picture he'd shown me all those weeks ago. She had a bottle in her hand too, and dropped to the space on the other side of me.

"You some of Von's family, or you from the neighborhood?" she asked, getting comfortable.

"Babs, this is Tristan's woman," Von spoke up. "You know he's gonna be mad he didn't get to introduce you first."

"I ain't worried about his ass," she laughed. "How you doing honey, I'm Barbara," she said, offering me her free hand. "Everybody calls me Babs – *Big Babs* for the real grown up folks."

"Pleased to meet you," I said, accepting her hand, and the

firm shake she offered before pulling me into a hug that was uncomfortably comfortable.

"You a pretty thing aren't you – with a sweet spirit. I can tell you got some *unfuckwittable* about you too. I like that."

"Me too BB," Von chimed in, reaching around me to give her a fist bump.

I… wasn't sure how I felt about this.

Not negative at all, it was just incredibly surreal, to be having a moment like that that wasn't… fabricated.

I wasn't measuring my words, wasn't keeping a cover intact, I was just… *being.*

Actually, I *did* know how I felt about it.

I felt fantastic.

"Ay, what the fuck is this?!" Tristan asked as he jogged up to us, still shirtless and dripping sweat. His locs were pulled up, brown skin glistening in the sun, all his ink on full display, and…

"Do y'all need some privacy?" Babs laughed, letting me know that the inappropriate place my thoughts had been going were more than evident on my face.

Shit.

In front of his mother, Temp?

"Chill, mama," Tristan scolded. "I thought I asked you to leave her be until I introduced you?"

She raised an eyebrow at him. "And *I* thought I was grown," she reminded. "And besides that, how was I supposed to know who she was – you hadn't introduced us yet."

That very valid point was one he couldn't argue against, so he let out a sigh. "Mama, this is Tempest. Tempest, this is my mother. Do not believe shit this one," he pointed at his mother, "Or *that one*," – he pointed at Von, who stuck her tongue out at him – "says about me."

"Neither has said anything bad …"

He grinned. "Oh well in that case believe it all."

"Just like a nigga," Von grumbled, sparking me and Babs to agree, which started a pleasant back and forth between the four of us that I could really barely believe.

But I'd accept it.

And bask in every moment of it.

After a while, Tristan gave me a sweaty ass kiss before he went to go get himself cleaned up. In the meantime, the food was ready, and after that, there was a big ass chorus of Stevie's *Happy Birthday* song, and gifts, and laughs, and all-around celebration of Kiara's day.

It was beautiful.

But I tried not to be in the way.

Tristan and I were still pretty damned new, and I didn't quite feel comfortable ingratiating myself with the family, but they insisted at every turn, not letting me tuck myself to the back. Even Kiara kept finding me, her hot pink braces on full display as she grinned every time our eyes met.

Especially when she opened her gift from me – a full range of candles and candle accessories all in hot pink, with her very own super-fruity super-girly *"KiKi Do You Love Me?"* scent, a nod to her inexplicably favorite rapper.

She was *thrilled.*

And I was thrilled that she was thrilled, and it was just... all around a good ass day.

I did manage to slip away once the cake was cut. Even with all the positives, so much "peopling" had me feeling drained, and I needed the break.

Needed the quiet moment.

When I walked into *Wax Poetic,* I smiled.

I hadn't given a single fuck about a candle when I bought this place, but now... being on this side of the doors made me feel... at peace. It was so different from the fear and apprehension I'd brought with me to the *Heights*.

I was different.

Not completely transformed, and I wasn't sure I ever would be, but I didn't *feel* like a "rose" anymore.

I ... felt like me.

It was almost sad.

Almost.

Maybe bittersweet was a better way to think of it. It stung a bit to realize I'd lost myself – the *me* that I'd known for so long. I had to let go of her though – had to let go of the coldness, the paranoia, the... programming.

I belonged solely to myself now.

I didn't have to follow anybody else's guidebook anymore.

I was *just* Tempest.

And *that* part was sweeter than anything I'd ever tasted.

A knock at the door pulled me from my musings, and I knew it was Tristan before I even turned around to look.

"Party over now?" I asked, once I'd unlocked the door to welcome him in, and he nodded.

"Kiara is off somewhere with her friends, Mama is with her homies from the neighborhood, Von is booed up with her man, so... shit, I came to be booed up too. I mean, if that's okay?"

"You know it is," I laughed, relishing the touch of his arms as he wrapped them around me, making me feel even more at home than I already did.

"Wait, what is this?" he asked, half-unwrapping himself from me to pick up a candle from the display nearby – the same one that had caught Dacia's attention when she was here. "*Neighborhood Hottie*?" he read from the label. "Seriously?"

I smirked as he pulled the wood top off, raising it to his nose.

"Oh *damn*, this really does smell like... *wow*," he laughed, smelling it again. "You really do fuck with me, huh?"

"I really do," I assured him, tucking my arms around his waist.

"Ah, so *Ms. Not Interested* is fully converted now?"

I nodded. "Yep. I can fully admit – I am *very,* very interested."

THE END.

ABOUT THE AUTHOR

Christina C. Jones is a modern romance novelist who has penned many love stories. She has earned a reputation as a storyteller who seamlessly weaves the complexities of modern life into captivating tales of black romance.

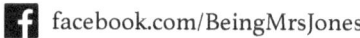 facebook.com/BeingMrsJones

IF YOU CAN SERIES

Catch Me If You Can

Release Me If You Can

Save Me If You Can

HIGH STAKES SERIES

Ante Up

King of Hearts: A Short Story Collection

Deuces Wild

EQUILIBRIUM SERIES

Love Notes

Grow Something: An Equilibrium Novelette

In Tandem

Frosted.Whipped.Buttered: An Equilibrium Short

Plus One: An Equilibrium Short

Bittersweet

Press Rewind: An Equilibrium Short

SWEET HEAT SERIES

Hints of Spice

A Dash of Heat

A Touch of Sugar

SERENDIPITIOUS SERIES

A Crazy Little Thing Called Love

Didn't Mean To Love You

Fall in Love Again

The Way Love Goes

Love You Forever

Something Like Love

CONNECTICUT KING SERIES (Collaboration with Love Belvin)

Love on the Highlight Reel (Book 2)

Determining Possession (Book 3)

Pass Interference (Book 6)

STRICTLY PROFESSIONAL

Strictly Professional

Unfinished Business

TRUTH AND LIES

The Truth: His Side, Her Side, and The Truth About Falling in Love

The Lies: The Lies We Tell About Life, Love, and Everything in Between

FRIENDS & LOVERS

Finding Forever

Chasing Commitment

ETERNALLY TETHERED

Haunted

Coveted

STANDALONES

Mine Tonight

Wonder

Equivalent Exchange

Love & Other Things

A Mutually Beneficial Agreement

Relationship Goals: a novella

Anonymous Acts (Five Star Enterprises)

AUDIOBOOKS:

Ante Up (High Stakes, Book 1)

Deuces Wild (High Stakes, Book 3)

I Think I Might Love You (Love Sisters, Book 1)

I Think I Might Need You (Love Sisters, Book 2)

Getting Schooled (Wright Brothers, Book 1)

Pulling Doubles (Wright Brothers, Book 2)

Bending the Rules (Wright Brothers, Book 3)

Inevitable Conclusions (Inevitable, Book 1)

Inevitable Seductions (Inevitable, Book 2)

Inevitable Addiction (Inevitable, Book 3)

Haunted (Eternally Tethered, Book 1)

Coveted (Eternally Tethered, Book 2)

The Culmination of Everything (Sugar Valley, Book 1)

Equivalent Exchange (Night Shift)

Wonder